UNITED ON VACATION

Linda Hoy was a teacher for almost ten years before becoming a full-time writer. She is the author of a number of books for young people, including *Nightmare Park; Your friend, Rebecca* and *Kiss.* She has also written an award-winning television play, *Emily.* She lives in Sheffield with an ancient cat called Scruffbag and enjoys heavy rock music, walking on the moors and scoffing vanilla slices.

Books by the same author

Emmeline Pankhurst
Haddock 'n' Chips
Nightmare Park
Ring of Death
Your Friend, Rebecca

For older readers

The Alternative Assembly Book
Kiss File JC110
Poems for Peace

UNITED ON VACATION

LINDA HOY

WALKER BOOKS
AND SUBSIDIARIES
LONDON • BOSTON • SYDNEY

First published 1994 by Walker Books Ltd
87 Vauxhall Walk, London SE11 5HJ

This edition published 1995

2 4 6 8 10 9 7 5 3

Printed in England

British Library Cataloguing in Publication Data
A catalogue record for this book is
available from the British Library.

ISBN 0-7445-3697-9

For Marcus –
a true supporter

CONTENTS

THE FIRST HALF

THE SECOND HALF

INJURY TIME

EXTRA TIME

THE
FIRST HALF

CHAPTER
ONE

"*You're listening to* Praise or Grumble *on Radio Sheffield and our next call is from George. Hello, George. Can you hear me?*"

"George! You're not still on that phone, are you?"

I place my hand over my ear. "Yes, Bob. Hello."

"*Is it Praise or Grumble, George?*"

"Praise, Bob."

"*And who's the Praise for, George?*"

"George! Your grandma might be trying to get through on the line."

"*Sorry, George. Did you say your grandma had a very good time? Did she go to the match with you?*"

"No, no. I heard it on the radio. I thought the commentary was very good."

"*Pleased you enjoyed it, George.*"

"It'll be costing us a fortune. Can't you get them to call you back?"

"*What was that, George. Did you say, 'And praise for the new left back...?'*"

"No, Bob. Praise for all the team. I mean, everyone's been praising John Little and it was Jo that scored but, well... I mean, it was team-work, wasn't it?"

"*Well then, it's Praise for United and Praise for the Radio Sheffield commentary. Thank you, George. You're listening to* Praise or Grumble, *and who've we got next...? Hello...*"

And a grumble from George's dad as he puts down the phone. "It all costs money, George. You must have been on at least ten minutes..."

Four and a half, actually.

"Time for your tea now, anyway."

Saturday teatime used to be full of Praise. Saturday was a table loaded with pickled onions and pepperoni, with spicy tortillas, hot garlic bread, deep fried chicken wings and barbecued spare ribs. Saturdays meant fresh cream cakes and trifle, chocolate gateau and ice-cream.

"Pass the dripping sandwiches, George, will you?"

And Saturdays meant football. Sitting down to tea after the match – that was Praise. A season ticket for the Kop, the atmosphere as the crowd thickened, building up on London Road, everyone heading towards the Lane. The rhythm of the football chants, assorted choirs mingling in the air:

> *United!*
> *United!*
> *United!*

"Pass the toast, George."

Red and white balloons soaring when the great team came racing out of the tunnel:

> *We are Blades men, super Blades men,*
> *we are Blades men, from the Lane...*

Feet stomping, crowd roaring, rising out of their seats whenever the ball bounded towards the goal...

> *And it's Sheffield United*
> *Sheffield United F.C. –*
> *are by far the greatest team*
> *the world has ever seen...*

"Don't pile so much lemon curd on your toast, George. It doesn't grow on trees, you know."

The whole crowd roaring with one voice whenever the great team scored. Thousands and thousands leaping to their feet. Shouting, hugging, red flares lighted, passed from hand to outstretched hand, shining winter faces glowing in its light. Illuminated scoreboard yelling *Goal! Goal! Goal!* as its computerized hands clapped together.

Now teatime on Saturdays means sandwiches: dripping sandwiches, lettuce sandwiches and lemon curd on toast. Saturday teatime is Grumble. I watch Mum as she dips the tea bag into Dad's cup – one … two … three … four seconds; then hers – one … two … three … four … five … six … seven … eight. Then she dunks it in my cup and leaves it.

"Time to move the car."

Just after dark, I tiptoe outside with Dad and we open the doors of the garage. We don't switch on the light. At the front of the garage, gleaming in the moonlight, stands my father's pride and joy – a shiny black Mercedes. Dad sits behind the steering wheel and I stand at the back.

"Ready!" Dad shouts.

And that's my signal to put my weight behind the car, ready to shove.

"Off we go."

Dad takes off the handbrake. I stand with both hands on the boot and then push hard. The car rolls smoothly and slowly, easing out of the garage, down the drive. Then Dad parks it in front of the wrought iron gates, beside the unlit Victorian lamp.

He climbs out, then wipes the boot where there are two palm prints covered in lemon curd. It doesn't really matter because he always cleans and polishes the car on Sundays. Then on Mondays we push it back and lock it up again.

You may think I must be extra strong to push such a big car. After all, I'm only twelve years old. But it's not as hard as it looks.

Our Mercedes doesn't have an engine.

I walk back into the house, then carry last week's papers upstairs to my room.

When we first bought the house, I thought my room was fantastic. It has red and white units stacked along the walls for housing my TV and video, my computer and all my computer games, my hi-fi and CD player, all my compact discs – even my own telephone socket. The door opposite leads to my very own bathroom with personal shower and bidet and even a sunken bath.

The problem is that the units now display nothing more than memories of happier days, the empty rectangles a sad reminder of how things used to be.

I've still got the bathroom, of course; we haven't sold that. But what we don't have any more is hot water. And I don't like cold baths. Even sitting on a freezing cold bidet is an experience I'd rather miss.

I do still have a desktop unit but since the central heating's been switched off, it's much too cold to sit at. Instead, I scramble under my United duvet with my scrapbook, scissors and glue-pot. Mum moans when I spill glue on the sheets, but it's usually dried by the time I go to bed.

I cut out the picture of Callum Welly performing his amazing match-winning penalty-save.

> *One Callum Welly –*
> *there's only one Callum Welly...*

I wipe the glue from the top of his head and from the edges of his shorts as I sit him squarely in the middle of the page.

> *...one Callum We-e-e-e-lly –*
> *there's only one Callum We-e-e-e-lly...*

The area behind the goal is littered with the shreds of a thousand red and white balloons.

"*And we seem to have a pitch invasion here. Yes, a mass onslaught from the Kop. A thousand red and white balloons are streaming down and soaring over the perimeter fence and ... yes, they're invading the pitch. The stewards are chasing after them but the wind's got behind the balloons now and they're straggling right across the Blackburn defence. Will the balloons put a stop to the game?*"

"George...?"

"*No. Alan Codger is dashing across to one of the white balloons. A bit short-sighted, there, I think, Alan. Never mind, he's heading it across to Jo, who's tackled by one of the Blackburn strikers, who begins a slalom with the balloon down towards the net. And Welly's poised on the edge of the six-yard box. And ... wow! What a wonderful save from..."*

"George...?"

I wipe the remaining paste off the goal-posts with my sleeve, then climb out of bed. "Hello."

"We're just off out for half an hour."

They always say half an hour. What they mean is that they're going to the pub for the evening.

"All right...?"

They always go out for a drink on Saturday night.

"OK."

They used to get me a babysitter but they can't afford one any more. It doesn't matter, anyway. I'm perfectly old enough now to stay in and look after myself.

"See you later, then. Don't stop up too late."

CHAPTER
TWO

After bringing my scrapbook up to date, I take
out my envelope full of raffle tickets.

BLADES FAMILY CLUB
GRAND CHRISTMAS DRAW

> ## 1st PRIZE
> Family holiday –
> two weeks in the sun

(Not much chance of winning that!)

> ## 2nd PRIZE
> 2 season tickets

(Just one would be fine.)

(But I'd be happy to win this instead.)

(Or this!)

"And Jo's got the ball now and he's intercepted by Palmer and Palmer's brought him down and ... this must be a foul and yes, yes, it's a penalty.

"Well, Sheffield Wednesday fans are far from pleased with that, but let's just have a quick comment here from our local United supporter... Well, George, what did you think of that decision?"

I used to go to every match at Bramall Lane. But that was when both my parents had jobs. Since their business went bankrupt, the nearest I've been to a football match has been listening on the radio. That's why I'm selling the raffle tickets.

IN ADDITION
we offer the following benefits,
linked to the amount of tickets
you can sell:

---

5 BOOKS SOLD
2 Kop seat tickets for a
Home League Match of your choice

10 BOOKS SOLD
4 Kop seat tickets for a
Home League Match of your choice

25 BOOKS SOLD
A Terrace Season Ticket

30 BOOKS SOLD
A Kop Season Ticket

60 BOOKS SOLD
A South Stand Season Ticket

I've read the words so often now they've become engraved upon my memory, as familiar as the opening music to *Match of the Day* or the words of a football chant.

I take out my pencil and recheck my multi-plication:

20 tickets in a book
5 books = 100 tickets
10 books = 200 tickets
25 books = 500 tickets
30 books = 600 tickets
60 books = 1,200 tickets

I recount the stubs of the five tickets that I've sold already.

Still a long way to go.

"And this is the club dressing-room ... if you'd like to go in here, George, and... Have you met Flostein Jo before?"

"Well, no, I haven't actually, but I've enjoyed watching him play."

"This is George, Jo. Come to look round the club."

"Pleased to meet you, George."

"Nice to meet you, Jo. And, if you don't mind my saying so, I was very impressed with the goal you scored this afternoon."

"Well, thanks very much, George. But, of course, we do have all the team to thank. I couldn't have done it on my own."

"Well, Jo, that's just what I said on Radio Sheffield. Teamwork. We have to praise all of the team..."

Drrrr. Drrrr. Drrrr. Drrrr.

I replace the tickets in their envelope as I go down to answer the phone.

"Hello."

"Hello, Gran. How are you?"

"Not very well. Is your mum there?"

"Can you shout up a bit? It's a bad line."

"No, no. I'm not fine. I've not been very well."

"Oh, I'm sorry to hear that."

"Is your mum there?"

"They've just popped out."

"No, no. It's not gout. It's my lumbago. Can I have a word with your mum?"

"They've just popped out."

"Sorry? Popped out of what?"

I listen as Gran complains about her lumbago and about the new disco that's opened next to the hamburger stall. Gran lives in Tenerife and doesn't have many people to talk to. My grandad died a few months ago.

"I wondered whether to come back home for Christmas..."

"Well..."

I hesitate because I'm not sure what Mum and Dad would think. Could we cope with the extra expense? We've no plans for a Christmas dinner this year or even a Christmas tree. But Grandma has plenty of money. I'm sure she'd chip in for a Christmas tree and a turkey.

"Well, it would be nice to see you."

"I bet you've grown..."

In fact, Gran would no doubt arrive loaded down with presents. When she saw how poor we were, she'd go out and buy us a new TV, boxes of Christmas crackers, chocolates and a video recorder.

"Do you think your mum and dad would mind?"

She'd wave her credit card around the Blades souvenir shop. Gran is – as my dad says – worth a bob or two.

"I'm sure they'd be very pleased."

She could probably run to a season ticket, an official United trainer's jacket and videos of all the season's games I've missed. "We'd all be very pleased indeed."

I'm just replacing the receiver when I hear a noise from the kitchen.

Of course, I'm in the house on my own. It isn't time yet for the pub to close, and when Mum and Dad come home, they normally use the front door.

Hanging inside the conservatory are some carriers filled with milk-bottle tops. I've been washing them out and saving them to make Christmas decorations. When anyone opens the kitchen door, the wind blows into the conservatory and rustles the silver paper. That's what I hear now.

I listen carefully. Everything's quiet again. I stop breathing. My heart's thumping and my hands are starting to sweat. It could be a window left open but, as the house is so cold, we normally keep the windows closed.

I hear the noise again. And something else. It could be footsteps. I think about running back upstairs, but if there's anyone there, they'd hear me. I don't want to have to hide under my bed or in the bathroom. I take a deep breath. *Come on, George*, I tell myself. *Be sensible*.

Once, when I was upstairs with my friend Rafiq, we heard a clatter from downstairs. "Burglars!" he hissed. We crept downstairs, gripping each other's arms, trying to scare each other and stifling giggles. Then we found a stray cat creeping round the conservatory. The kitchen window had been left open and the cat had jumped inside.

Being scared was fun when Rafiq was here. It feels different now I'm on my own. I take a deep breath.

I give the door to the lounge a little push, then peer round into the darkness. I can't see anything. I reach tentatively round the corner and turn up the dimmer switch.

I don't see anything at first. I'm just about to let out my breath when I notice a shape. There's someone standing flat against the wall, behind the unit where the TV and video used to be. My mouth drops open. My stomach turns a somersault. I think about running back upstairs. I try to run, in fact, but when I tell my feet to move, they seem to be stuck in pots of glue.

The figure turns slightly. It's a man. He sees me and, when he realizes that I've seen him, steps out into the open. He's wearing a grey suit and holding a very large briefcase. He doesn't look like a burglar or a murderer. We stand for a couple of seconds, staring at each other. He looks quite respectable. Perhaps he's a bailiff or a debt collector. Dad used to say how the bailiffs would come to repossess our things – but that was when we still had things for the bailiffs to repossess.

Both of us seem equally surprised. After a while, he says, "Hello."

Of course, he could be a murderer. He could be a terrorist looking for hostages.

"Hello." My voice sounds strange and squeaky. I still have my raffle tickets and my Biro in my hand and I realize that they're getting wet with sweat.

The man bites his lip as though he's thinking hard. "Who are you?" he asks.

I don't know whether I ought to tell him. It ought to be me that's asking questions but I can't think what to say.

There's another silence. He looks over my shoulder towards the hall. "Is there anyone else here?"

I don't say anything. I don't want him to

know we're on our own. And I don't want to get Mum and Dad into trouble for going out and leaving me. He could be from the Social Services or the NSPCC.

"I'm sorry," he says.

I open my mouth to try and ask him who he is but the words get squashed inside my throat.

"I'm sorry," he says again. "Sorry to bother you – I mean. I'm..." He looks around the room uncertainly. "I'm supposed to be a ... well, there doesn't seem anything here to take but, well ... I'm supposed to be a burglar."

I always thought burglars were young, fit, teenage hooligans. Or men with black Balaclavas and Cockney accents. This man's quite old. He sounds respectable and he's better dressed than my father.

"You're the only house without an alarm," he explains.

I nod. "We used to have one," I squeak. "Only we had to sell it."

We both gaze around the room at the empty hi-fi unit, the glass-fronted display cabinet with its shelves of unpaid bills and the padded cocktail bar with its half-empty bottle of peapod wine.

"We've nothing left to steal."

He nods. He stares at the empty video and TV unit. "Where's your telly and your video?"

"We've had to sell them. We used to have a satellite."

26

"Oh." He looks sympathetic. "I've got loads of tellies at home. I've got a garage full." He pauses. "I could've…" I think for a moment he might be offering to bring us one round, but he seems to think better of it.

"Anyway," he says, "I'm sorry."

There's another awkward silence. I don't know what you're supposed to talk to a burglar about. It doesn't seem right to offer him a cup of tea.

He glances at my sweatshirt. "A United fan, eh?"

I nod.

"Did you get down today then? Blackburn?"

"No." I shake my head. "I did hear it on the radio, though. I was on *Praise or Grumble*. I don't know if you heard it?"

He shakes his head.

"I can't afford the tickets now."

There's another pause. Suddenly, I remember the envelope of raffle tickets, still folded and sweating in my palm. "I've been selling raffle tickets for the club," I explain. "If I sell enough, I can get a free ticket for next season."

The burglar nods.

"There's some good prizes. There's a fortnight's holiday and a season ticket…" It seems like a shot in the dark, but why not? I give him a little smile. "It's a very good raffle. If you think you might be interested…" I hold out the book. "They're ten tickets for five pounds."

The burglar takes the book and reads through the list of prizes. "Mm. Well, I would like to buy some but... You see, I'd prefer not to put my name and address down, really."

Of course. He can't just walk out, leaving his name and address behind.

He reads through the tickets again. "It does look good though. I'll tell you what. I am sorry about, you know, all this." He waves his hand vaguely round the living-room. I don't know if he's sorry for being a burglar or sorry that we've nothing left to steal. "I'll buy some tickets and put your name down, eh? Give you a chance to win."

CHAPTER
THREE

End of break time in the art room and I'm
gloating at the rows of neatly washed paint-
brushes standing to attention in their rack
beside the sink.

"Well, that's very good of you, George. You
have worked hard."

I smile sweetly at the paint trays, washed
and scrubbed, tottering lopsidedly.

"It was very kind of you to stay in and tidy
up. It must have taken you nearly all break."

Of course, Miss hasn't yet noticed the sink.
It seemed to get itself blocked with bits of
paper towels and wodges of compressed
powder paint. And then I couldn't turn the
tap off.

"I wondered…" I try to sound as if I'm
offering Miss a special favour. "I wondered …
if you might like to buy a raffle ticket." I give

Miss Currie an angelic smile as I sidle across to block her view of the dirty paint water rising to the top of the sink.

"Well, I'll just have a look in my purse."

In Science we've been studying the spectrum. When you put all the colours of the rainbow on a disc and then whirr it round, the colours merge together and become white.

I glance at the liquid beginning to trickle down the legs of the sink and onto the art room floor. When you mix all the colours of the spectrum in a sink, I notice, they don't come out white at all. They come out black. Dirty, smelly, inky black.

"They're only two for a pound, Miss. Or – " I suggest hopefully – "three for one pound fifty."

I sit with my sandwiches on the grass behind the school car park and inspect my raffle ticket book. With my mouth full of bread and dripping, I take out my pencil and check the familiar sums:

20 tickets in a book
5 books = 100 tickets…
60 books = 1,200 tickets

I recount the stubs of the fifteen tickets that I've sold already.

Still a long way to go.

"And can you tell our listeners what you think of the Blades Christmas raffle so far, George.

Is it Praise or Grumble?"

"Well, it's Praise for the raffle itself. I mean, I think the prizes, Bob, are excellent. But it's Grumble for the price of the tickets. I mean, 50p. Well, it's a lot of money nowadays…"

It wasn't a lot of money for Mr Woodward, the chairman of our school governors. I didn't know who he was, of course, when I saw his 2CV turn into the car park. But when I saw his Blades on Tour car flag and United window sticker, I could sense a potential customer. I clutched my book of raffle tickets and followed him into school.

At first, I thought he was a workman. He had holes in his jeans, a pair of scuffed trainers and a shabby leather jacket. He stood in the dining hall, looking lost.

"Can I help you?" I asked, smiling my sweet smile.

He nodded. "I'm looking for the head's office."

Mr Dooley's office is actually only a very short distance from the dining hall, but not the way we went.

"Follow me," I said, striding in the opposite direction. I led him towards the changing rooms, the gym and the all-weather pitch.

"This is the football pitch," I pointed out as though he was in danger of mistaking it for a table tennis table or a swimming pool.

"Do you play football?"

I shook my head. "No, but I support United."

Of course, that kept the conversation in full flow as I conducted him round the music block, directed him towards the drama studio and almost booted him into the computer room. By the time we'd threaded our way through Textiles, I'd given him the whole sob story of my financial plight, my thwarted hopes of ever going to see my favourite team again and had already introduced the subject of the raffle. It was then that I spied Mr Dooley, the headmaster, wheeling his way towards us through the pottery studio.

"The tickets are only fifty p," I hurriedly explained. "Or it's – " I had worked extra hard to earn this – "five for two pounds fifty."

"I'll have five," he offered, reaching for his wallet.

"Ah, Mr Woodward!" the head exclaimed. "There you are!"

He turned around and glared at me. "What are you doing?" he asked suspiciously as he saw me pocketing the cash.

I said nothing.

"This young man here's been very helpful," Mr Woodward explained. "He's just given me a conducted tour – all around the school."

"Hmmm." Mr Dooley didn't look too pleased. I tore off the next five tickets and held up my pencil, ready to fill in the counterfoils. "What address shall I put?"

Mr Woodward smiled at me. "Put your own name down, lad," he told me. "Give yourself a chance to win a prize, eh?"

I used to go to a private school. I used to wear a uniform with a blazer, white shirt and tie. I used to carry my books in a leather briefcase with my initials in brass letters on the side.

My dad used to take me to school each morning in the black Mercedes. Then, later, Mum would pick me up in her red Toyota MR2. My dad had to sell his car engine to help pay off the school fees.

He'd have got more money, of course, if he'd sold the whole of the car but he didn't want the neighbours to notice that we'd hit hard times. That's why we wheel the empty car out every Saturday, stand it on the drive for two days, clean and polish it, then wheel it back.

Now I come to Hartfield Comprehensive on the bus. I don't mind because I've made lots of new friends. The one thing I do mind, though, is going without a school dinner.

Hartfield is a multi-ethnic school so they have curry and chips, pasties and samosas, pizza, spaghetti and sweet and sour pork. They also have apple pie and custard, jammy doughnuts, fruit salad, treacle roly-poly or chocolate cake for pudding.

I say *they have* because I sit behind the car park with my dripping sandwiches. When I complained that I was missing out on vitamins, Mum made me dripping sandwiches with lettuce.

What I miss is the atmosphere in the dining hall – the smell of hot, tasty food, the laughter and conversation. If I went on free school dinners, of course, I could eat anything I wanted.

"No one minds," I explained to Mum. "Lots of the kids have single parents. Lots of them have parents out of work."

But Mum just shook her head. "We have certain standards to keep up, George," she said. "And up to now, touch wood, we've been keeping our heads above water."

CHAPTER FOUR

Mum and Dad are horrified to hear that Grandma wants to come home for Christmas.

"How can we feed anyone else?" Mum shakes her head at the blue airmail letter lying on the shelf where the microwave used to be. "We've already decided that we can't afford a Christmas dinner."

"She's much better off where she is," says Dad. "It's nice and warm in Tenerife. She'll have forgotten what an English winter's like. And she's not really well enough to travel."

I haven't mentioned that I told Gran on the phone it would be very nice to see her.

"She'll expect a Christmas tree and turkey, sherry and gin and chocolate liqueurs," Mum complains.

"She'll certainly expect a TV and a video," moans Dad.

"She'll understand," I interrupt. "If you explain about—"

Dad shakes his head. "Grandma thinks unemployment just affects miners and people in the steelworks. There's been no recession in Tenerife." He pauses. "Grandma thinks I'm still in full employment."

"Well, let's write to her and explain," I suggest. "Tell her that she'll be very welcome but she'll have to bring her own turkey."

I went round to Rafiq's house a few days ago. Rafiq is a friend I've made at my new school. He lives in a terraced house near Bramall Lane with his mother and father, his uncle and several brothers and sisters. Their business isn't doing very well. They own two taxis and a corner shop. They have to run the taxis all night long and keep the shop open until 9.30 every evening. Their house is small. They haven't got a swimming pool and they only have one bathroom but they have much more money than we do.

Rafiq and his brothers, for instance, can always afford a ticket for the football. When I went round, his mum gave me sweets and lots of cake and the fridge was stacked with cola and lemonade. I could smell their meal cooking in a great big pan. There'll be no lemon curd on toast for Rafiq. And they have satellite TV.

I tried to explain about this to my father. "If we sold our house," I explained for the umpteenth time, "and bought somewhere smaller – near Bramall Lane, for instance – then we'd have lots of spare cash. We could go on holiday, go out for meals, visit Grandma in Tenerife…"

Dad just shook his head. "Look, George," he said, lighting a cigarette. "Maybe Rafiq and his family have never known anything better. We have. We've always been up in the premier division." He inhaled on his cigarette. You see, that's another way we could save lots of money, but I'm fed up with telling him that. "Let's face it, George. You wouldn't want to support a team that had been relegated to the first or the second division. Would you?"

I stared at him blankly. I didn't know what to say. What if United were relegated? The threat has been there ever since they entered the premier division. I've heard older people talking about the horrors of the past when United were relegated to the second and then to the third division. Other supporters have the excitement of wondering whether their team might win the League or win the Cup. United fans have the excitement of wondering where we'll be next season. And of course we'd all be sorry if they went down. It would be a sad, sad, sad, sad day.

But would I stop supporting them?

Anyway, what my father hasn't noticed is that our family were relegated a couple of seasons ago. When Mum and Dad talk about keeping our heads above water, they really mean that they're struggling to hang on to a lifestyle we can no longer afford. Like a third division team that owns the best ground in the country but can't afford a single decent player.

Or even a pair of boots.

CHAPTER
FIVE

It's just two weeks before Christmas when I hear the news from Bramall Lane.

Mum and Dad are eating breakfast in the conservatory. Even though neither of them has a job, they still get up at the same time every day. Dad wears his suit and a smartly pressed white shirt and tie. He leaves the house at 8.30 every morning, carrying his briefcase and umbrella. I don't know where he goes. He signs on once a week and he sometimes goes to the library to look for any jobs there in the newspapers. It's a long time, though, since he applied for one; we can't even afford the stamps.

I stir my third-hand tea bag round my mug, squeezing it against the edges to try and make the hot water turn brown.

"Pass the dripping please, George."

I wrinkle my knife across the dripping before passing the basin to Dad. I glance around the table for some toast.

Dad switches on the radio.

"It's Monday, December seventeenth, and you're listening to Radio Sheffield.

"Well, there'll be lots of happy, smiling faces around the South Yorkshire area today because this is the day that United are announcing the winners of their grand Christmas Draw. Winners will be notified by post and we'll have more details of who's won those magnificent prizes later in the day. Now over to…"

The post normally arrives while we're having breakfast. My heart starts puttering. I stand up from the table and walk through the lounge into the hall.

There's a pile of letters on the mat. I pick them up with shaking hands: one from Gran in Tenerife, a red phone bill, a brown envelope from the tax office and one of the long white envelopes with LORD CHANCELLOR'S OFFICE typed across the top. These letters, I know from sad experience, are the kind that involve the jar of lemon curd being scraped so clean you could read a football programme through it.

But it's the fifth letter that makes me stop and hold my breath. It has a crest of crossed blades in the top left-hand corner and my name typed neatly and blackly in the centre. There's no computer label so it's not a letter sent to everyone. It's a special letter with a first class stamp – a special letter for me.

I might have won the raffle: I could have won two season tickets or the one hundred pound Blades souvenir shop voucher; it could be the VIP day at the Lane. I know it won't be a South Stand season ticket because I didn't sell enough books for one of those.

I dare not open the letter. I walk back into the kitchen and stand my envelope on the table, leaning it against the lemon curd. I can't bear to open it. While the envelope is sealed, any of the prizes could be mine. I think about the VIP day – meeting the team in the dressing room and sitting in the Radio Sheffield commentary box.

"And what do you think of the raffle now, George, is it Praise or Grumble?"

"Praise, Bob. Praise all the way. I'm having a wonderful time and I just want to say how much I appreciate United for organizing this."

I could have won the holiday or a ticket for the Kop. But once I open the envelope... Of course, the letter might be telling me I haven't won anything at all.

"Are you all right, George?"

Perhaps I should have some more toast. I reach across for the lemon curd, but there's a fluttering in my stomach like a cluster of red and white balloons being released before a match. The envelope stares at me from its position between the lemon curd and the toast rack, staring like an open goal.

"More dripping, George?"

It winks and shines, gleaming like a ray of sunlight in the fog.

I can't put it off. I pick up the envelope, weighing it in my hand, struggling to click my eyes onto X-ray vision to see through to its inside. Then I reach across for the breadknife. I must be careful. I mustn't tear the contents because inside could be a souvenir shop voucher, a ticket for a holiday, two season tickets, a... I'm bouncing up and down on my seat, almost dropping the breadknife.

"Are you feeling all right, George?"

I ease the blade into the top of the envelope and begin to tear it across, fingers fumbling, covering the precious envelope in lemon curd and dripping.

"George...?"

Inside is a letter. Just a letter. No tickets. I tip the torn envelope upside down and shake it, just to make sure. No voucher. No cash. Just a letter. I open it with shaking fingers:

```
Dear Sir,
```

I can't hold the paper still enough to read.

"George? Is anything wrong?"

I try to read the ending first and there's something about a holiday. A holiday! A holiday! I bounce again like an overinflated football. I must keep still. I force myself to start again and read the letter properly. I read it from the beginning.

> Dear Sir,
>
> We are very pleased to inform you that you have won the star prize in the United Grand Christmas Draw.

"Star Prize! Whoooooooo!"

> Your prize is a holiday for you and your family for two weeks...

"Family holiday! Whooooooo!!"

> ...on an island in the sun.

"Island in the sun! Whoooooooooooooooo!!!" I leap out of my seat and jump around the kitchen. I piston my fists in the air the way Jo does when he's scored a winning goal. "Star prize! It's the star prize!" I explain to my father, still peering over last week's newspaper, his mouth full of toast and dripping.

"I've won the holiday!" I explain to my mum, manoeuvring her second tea bag of the morning from Dad's mug into hers. "I've won the star prize! The island in the sun!"

I skip around the living-room, I bunny jump along the settee and then leap outside, and skip around the empty swimming pool. "I've won the holiday," I sing. "I've won the holiday!"

43

I see the cracked, leaf-splattered empty pool transformed into a sunshine paradise – palm trees, sunbeds, ice-cream, beach umbrellas, hot, hot, hot, hot sun. I think of hotel food, three meals every day. Serve yourself buffet, go back as often as you like: croissants and sausages for breakfast, hot food, proper puddings. It did say a hotel, didn't it? Did it mention full board? Hope so. Must have done.

As I skip back into the conservatory, Mum and Dad are still staring at me in disbelief. I grin at them like a maniac before snatching the toast from the toast rack and starting to juggle – first two, and then three slices – all around the table, past the bowls of peapod wine fermenting on the floor.

Dad finally puts down his newspaper. "George," he looks at me with concern. "Are you all right?"

My juggling skills are not quite as good as I thought and I suddenly invent a completely new flavour of wine: toasted lemon curd and peapod.

"George, did I hear you say something about a holiday?"

CHAPTER
SIX

I am the one who has rescued our family, I tell myself as I empty out the contents of my Blades football money box. I am the one who has placed our family up where we belong, back in the premier division.

I replace the precious letter in its envelope and stash it safely in the zip pocket of my red and white striped sportsbag. I place the meagre savings from my money box inside my wallet with its gold embossed Blades crest. This is the kind of item I bought regularly with my pocket money in the good old days when we were rich.

I've been walking to school recently to save on bus fare, but today I can't wait to tell everyone the news. I sit on the top deck with Rafiq, Assam and Ben.

"What did the letter say?" asks Rafiq.

"Here – have a look." I pass him the letter. "Don't pass it all round the bus, though." I don't want it to get torn. I'm thinking I might frame the letter later and display it on my wall with the holiday photos and the airline tickets.

By the time we arrive in the form room, everybody's heard about the holiday. Rafiq has caught up with Mr Carr, our form teacher, and told him the news even before he's walked inside the classroom. The United letter has already been passed around more people than a lighted flare after a goal.

"Well now," says Mr Carr after registration, "perhaps you'd like to come out to the front, George, and tell us all about the holiday and how you came to win the prize?"

Of course, not everyone in the class is interested. Not everyone is a loyal Blades fan. Hartcliff Comprehensive contains a rather large nest of Owls – supporters of our arch enemies. We have the great misfortune to have some of them in our class.

I walk out to the front, making a discreet rude gesture at the nest of hooting Owls supporters perched over towards the window. I clutch my now slightly crumpled letter as I tell the class about the raffle tickets and how hard I've had to work to sell so many. I explain how well I supported United in the days before the recession; I explain why I wanted to try and win some tickets for next season. I don't explain why two weeks in the sun might just help our family to survive the worst winter of our lives.

At lunch-time, I celebrate the occasion with two salami pizzas, three helpings of chips, two ladlings of baked beans and a sausage roll. I sit at a table in the dining-room, surrounded by warmth, by the aroma of freshly cooked food and by a circle of friendly, chattering school pals.

"Well, George, and what do you think about the school dinner today? Is it Praise or Grumble?"

"Praise, Bob. Praise all the way. I think the choice is excellent. The food's nice and hot and this deep pan salami pizza is especially spicy with a beautiful spongy texture..."

For pudding I have hot treacle tart and custard, an apple doughnut and a flapjack. For I have scored the winning goal, that's what I tell myself – in the last few minutes before the whistle when everything seemed to be lost. Of course, the holiday won't get Dad a job and it won't even help to pay the mortgage but, as football managers have been known to remark so often, it's your ability to keep up the spirit of the team that determines whether you win or lose.

After school, I decide to give myself another treat. I stay on the bus right down Abbeydale

Road and get off just before town. I walk down Woodhead Road, towards the familiar floodlights, and make my way through the car park towards the towering concrete South Stand. I pass the social club, the executive suite, the players' entrance, the pools office, the directors' suite and the ticket office to arrive at the famous Blades souvenir shop.

I still have some money left – school dinners aren't that expensive – but my combined savings of the last few months can't really buy me much. The main items on display are this season's Blades track suits and trainers' jackets, but I can't afford any of those. There are official United club sweatshirts and hooded tops, but those are much too expensive. I take out my wallet to recount my money, but then my eye just catches a rail marked:

BARGAIN SALE OF SUMMER STOCK

And right at the front in brilliant yellow is the very item that I need, the ideal garment for my holiday. A big bold T-shirt with the SUFC crossed blades on the chest, a silhouette of green palm trees, a sun parasol, a beach towel, a deck chair and printed all around it:

SHEFFIELD UNITED ON VACATION

Straight away I see myself wearing that very T-shirt, lazing on my sunbed, licking a strawberry ice-cream and sipping a tropical fruit drink. Scattered around me are sunglasses, suntan oil and a pile of football magazines.

The price has been reduced because the summer T-shirts are all last season's stock. But it does mean I can afford it. I pounce on the T-shirt, the last one, I notice, just my size – well, a little bit large but I'm not intending to get any thinner after two weeks of hotel food – and I carry it over to the counter.

In the old days, we used to celebrate special occasions by going out for a meal. When it was my turn, I'd choose the Stancliffe Diner. I used to like their french fries and barbecued spareribs with chicken wings and sour cream dip. Then I used to have non-alcoholic cocktails followed by Death by Chocolate.

It occurs to me, as I walk home, that Mum and Dad might celebrate today. Probably not by going out for a meal, but something special for tea perhaps. I've seen special occasions on TV where the whole street has been decked out with bunting and welcome-home flags. I don't suppose that's likely either, but it does occur to me they might have switched on the central heating or put fairy lights round the front door.

But the house is just as cold as ever. There is no smell of cooking. No Christmas tree. No fairy lights. No WELCOME HOME, GEORGE bunting. In fact, when I walk into the kitchen, Mum and Dad look more depressed than ever.

"How about this, then?" I open the United carrier and remove the bright yellow T-shirt, holding it out for them both to see. "I've bought it for the holiday."

Mum frowns at the deck chair and the silhouetted palm trees. She scowls at the parasol and the beach towel. There's a moment's pause. "Can you take it back?" she asks.

My heart sinks. Why would I want to take it back? It said sale goods couldn't be exchanged, anyway. "No," I tell her, puzzled. I can't understand what I've done wrong. "No, I can't."

She looks across at Dad. "Sit down, George," he tells me. "We've got some bad news for you."

My spirits sag. My excitement deflates like a punctured football. We've had so much bad news in the last twelve months, I can't think of anything else that can happen. Perhaps my grandma's died.

I sink down into a chair.

Mum holds out the Tenerife airmail letter. "We've been talking about your grandma." She purses her lips into the shape of a smile. "She seems to have made up her mind that she's coming home for Christmas."

Well, at least she's still alive.

"Your gran's an old woman now, George," Mum carries on. "She's in her seventies. We'll have to try and give her a good time."

50

There's a small knot hardening in my stomach. It hardens tighter when Dad picks up his cigarettes from the shelf where the ice-cream maker and the coffee machine used to sit.

"You never know, it could be the last time we ever see your grandma."

The dark relegation zone of poverty has hung over us since my parents' business first began to go downhill. That was a long time ago. Mum and Dad kept saying how things would get better. We'd be all right, they said, if we could only get an extra bank loan. We'd be all right, they said, if we could only get a second mortgage. We'd be all right, my dad said, if he could only find another job.

"Anyway, George," Mum explains, "we've been talking things over."

I suggested, right from the start, that we should sell the house and buy somewhere smaller. We could have a garden to grow our own vegetables instead of an empty swimming pool. My dad could give up smoking. He could sell the Mercedes, I suggested, and buy a second-hand bike.

But because I'm only twelve years old, none of my suggestions count for anything at all.

I gaze around the kitchen at the empty mahogany kitchen units, at the empty space where the automatic washer and tumble-drier used to be stacked.

Mum gives me an empty smile. A smile with

an empty space where something else used to be but I can't remember what.

There's an ominous pause.

"Your father and I have decided that we can't afford to go on holiday."

What does she mean?

"But I've won the holiday," I protest. "We don't have to pay for it."

Mum just shakes her head. "We can use the money for something else. We've got another mouth to feed now at Christmas. We've got to provide for your grandma."

I stare at her in disbelief. What ever is she saying?

Mum looks across at Dad, waiting for him to explain.

Dad blows out his match and inhales on his cigarette. "I'm sorry, George," he tells me. "I know how excited you were, but well ... we just can't afford to go. If we sell the holiday, you see, then we can use the money over Christmas. We can have a proper Christmas dinner, switch the heating on, rent a telly for a few weeks."

I can't believe it. I really cannot believe it. I stare open-mouthed at my father.

"I thought you might be disappointed," says Dad.

Disappointed?

I think of the hours I worked, the tickets I sold. I think of how proud I was when I stood up this morning at school and showed the whole class the letter. I think of the island in the sun, the palm trees, the sand, the hot sun blazing down. I think of the hotel room. I think of hot showers and three-course meals in the restaurant.

The knot in my stomach turns to a lump inside my throat. I fight back the tears which are clouding up my eyes.

I stare down at the yellow T-shirt.

My mouth opens and closes but I just can't think of anything to say.

CHAPTER SEVEN

"This boy is seriously ill," says the doctor, removing her stethoscope. *"There's really very little hope."*

"Oh, no. You don't mean, he's—"

"A constant diet of lemon curd, toast and dripping is no good for a growing boy. And the pneumonia has been caused by sleeping in a freezing cold bedroom. You don't think you could... I mean, the only real hope would be for him to go away for a holiday somewhere in the sun. You don't think there's any chance of...?"

I rummage around the bottle bank but this week there seems to be nothing but cider and lemonade bottles. Surely we're not the only ones who can't afford wine nowadays.

"Look, George, we've had another letter from Grandma. She's found out that we're

thinking of selling the holiday and she's sent us a cheque. A huge cheque. An enormous one actually. That means we can afford to go on holiday and have a wonderful Christmas..."

The bottle bank isn't emptied very often, so every few weeks there's an overflow of wine and pop bottles, leaning against the skip. Other people bring their bottles for recycling; I come here to recycle them back. I look for wine bottles with nice, fancy labels. When I get home, Dad washes them out and fills them with his home-made peapod and potato wine.

"You see, Grandma, that Christmas jumper's much too large because I'm only half the size I used to be. I'm wasting away. All of us are starving."

I fill my bag with the best of the cider bottles, then rummage around the polythene bags, sorting through last week's papers. Why does no one ever recycle *Shoot* or *Goal*, I wonder. Never mind, even the *Sheffield Star* and the *Daily Mirror* sometimes have decent football. There's a couple of Owls programmes but I wouldn't want to contaminate my hands by touching those.

"I won this holiday in a competition, Grandma, but now we're selling it so that you can be happy at Christmas. We just want you to have a good time.

"What? Change our minds, Grandma? Go away on holiday with extra spending money from

you? Are you really sure you can afford it?"

I look over my shoulder to check there's no one watching before opening my sports bag and stuffing the papers inside. Then I sling the bag over my shoulder and set off up the hill.

I stop and blow on my fingers to defrost them. The weather is extra cold this week. There are splits in my trainers and icicles sprouting through my socks. There are holes in my jeans and the wind is whistling down my legs. I can't stop thinking about the island in the sun.

Mum and Dad have placed an advert in the paper. They've described the holiday as an unwanted prize.

An unwanted prize!

I plunge my hands back inside my pockets. Even they have holes.

I know why my parents want to be nice to Grandma: they think she might die soon and leave them all her money. People do die when they're Grandma's age, but some of them don't. Some people live to be a hundred.

FOR SALE
HOLIDAY IN DJERBA
First Two Weeks in Jan.
4 ☆ Beach Hotel

No reasonable offer refused
Phone any time   Unwanted prize

Mum has cut out the advert from the paper and placed it by the phone. Beside it, there's a notepad and pen so we can write down people's names and the amount they're prepared to pay.

At first, I allow myself to hope that nobody will want the holiday. Perhaps nobody will see the ad and, anyway, no one will be able to take two weeks off in January.

But, of course, the phone rings constantly and the list of names beside the telephone grows longer and longer. "Well, we have got one or two other people interested." I hear Mum's businesslike voice. "If you'd like to leave your name and number, we'll give you a ring in a couple of days."

Each time I walk through the hall, I turn my head away from the phone, but this does not erase the advert from my mind. The words scream out louder than ever. What I keep saying to myself over and over again is that the holiday was not unwanted. I wanted that holiday; I wanted it very, very, very, very much.

On Saturday evening there's a call from Rafiq. "I thought I might come over and see you," he says. "Will that be all right?"

I seldom invite anyone from school back to our house nowadays, but I've been several times to Rafiq's house so I don't know what to say. "It's a bit cold round here," I explain.

"The heating's not working."

"That's all right. I'll wear an extra jumper."

"And my computer's had to go back to the shop."

"That's all right. I don't mind watching telly."

"Well, actually, we haven't got a telly – not at the moment."

"Well, it doesn't matter, does it? We can have a game of Scrabble."

I think of the empty kitchen. We've got nothing to offer Rafiq – no biscuits, no crisps. We don't even have a can of Coke. "We haven't got much food…"

"Look," he explains. "I just want to get out for a couple of hours."

In the background, I can hear raised voices. I don't know what they're arguing about because Rafiq's family speak Bengali.

"Is that all right?"

"Of course. Yes. It'll be fine."

There's an extra advantage in the visit from Rafiq because it means my parents can go to the pub.

Ever since the visit from the Blades-supporting burglar, Mum and Dad have been reluctant to go out and leave me. This has meant long Saturday nights with the two of them, sitting with dismal faces, filling in last week's crossword in the paper. Sometimes, for a bit of light relief, they've read out last week's horoscopes and weather forecast.

I've tried to keep out of the way.

Mum and Dad wait until Rafiq arrives before they leave the house.

"Here's the notepad," Mum explains.

I take a deep breath.

"These are the different columns."

I glance down at the headings:

NAME:	PHONE NO:	PRICE:

but I intend to walk past and ignore them. I shall leave the phone ringing away to itself. It can ring all day and all night long. I refuse to answer. I refuse to spell out the attractions of our so-called unwanted holiday. I refuse to take the name and number of potential customers and offer to call them back.

"I've brought my Scrabble," says Rafiq.

"We'll go upstairs. We'll be a bit warmer under the duvet," I tell him. "What was the argument about?"

Rafiq sighs. "The usual thing. What do all families moan about? Money."

We set out the Scrabble on top of the duvet and try not to upset the letters every time we move. Downstairs, the telephone rings on and on and on. It's a pity that we had to sell the answerphone.

After nine-thirty, the ringing eases off and we decide to go downstairs and make ourselves some toast. Just when we're walking through the hall, however, the phone awakes and springs back into life.

I growl at the receiver, then snatch it out of its cradle. "Yes...!?" I snarl.

It's a woman's voice. "I'm phoning about the holiday."

I say nothing.

"I phoned earlier but there didn't seem to be anyone in."

Silence. I glare at the receiver. The woman sounds very, very old. She ought to be in bed by now.

"It sounds just what I need for my parents..."

Parents? She sounds like a great-great-grandmother herself.

"I phoned yesterday and left an offer but, well, I was thinking I could afford to pay a bit more. I mean, it would be lovely for Mum and Dad to get away. It would make such a nice Christmas present. So I thought that..."

Her parents must be far too old to go on holiday. Whatever is she on about?

"I was hoping I could clinch it over the phone. I was thinking ... would an extra two hundred pounds be enough?"

An extra two hundred pounds. Extra two hundred.

"There's nobody in," I tell her.

"Well…" She sounds a bit confused. "You're in, aren't you?"

I could tell her I'm a burglar. The famous brown-suited, empty-briefcased burglar. "I'm not selling the holiday," I explain. "It's my parents. They're selling it."

"Well, would you take my name down, please, and ask them to call me back?"

I sigh deeply.

"The name's Street. Miss Cherry Street."

I grudgingly pick up the pen by the phone.

"Only, if it's no longer available, I'll go down to the travel agent first thing on Monday morning. They do need to go away somewhere, you see, and I thought I'd…"

"Tell her they wouldn't like it," suggests Rafiq.

"I don't think they'd like it."

"Sorry?"

"It'll be too hot."

Of course, I've been telling Rafiq all about my disappointment with the holiday. "It'll be very hot. It won't be suitable for old people."

"Well, that's the idea, to send them somewhere warm. They need to get out of the cold."

"Tell her about the camels."

"And it'll be too foreign for them. It's like a desert island – all camels and palm trees."

"It sounds lovely."

"Tell her about the noise."

"And it's very noisy. There's a disco – just next to the hamburger stall. It'll keep them awake at night."

"No, no, I don't think so. They're quite deaf, you see. It'll take a lot more than a disco to keep them awake."

"Tell her about the foreign food."

"And you can't buy English food. It's all..." Whatever do they eat in Africa?

"Chapatis," suggests Rafiq.

"It's all chapatis and onion bhajees and..." I'm not too sure. "And coconuts."

"Well, they both like a bit of adventure."

"Tell her about the sharks."

"And there's all the sharks. It isn't safe to swim in the sea. There are man-eating sharks that—"

"Well, that won't matter. They're not too keen on swimming. A nice boat trip round the bay – that's more their cup of tea."

Sigh. I glance at Rafiq in desperation.

He shrugs his shoulders.

Silence.

"Would you like to take my number?"

CHAPTER EIGHT

When I arrive home from school on Monday,
I notice a very, very, very old car parked inside
our wrought iron gates. There seems to be
someone huddled on the back seat, but I don't
investigate too closely because our front door
is open and there's someone standing in the
hall.

My heart slides lower and lower down
through my stomach, into my legs and inside
my leaking trainers. It has to be Miss Cherry
Street. Has to be because she's holding something that looks suspiciously like our
unwanted holiday tickets in her hand. My
mother is counting a wad of twenty pound
notes with a big smile on her face. She looks a
lot more cheerful than I've seen her for a long,
long time.

Miss Street seems even older than she

sounded on the phone. She wears glasses and has long grey hair tied back in a plait. Mum stares pityingly at her ancient black duffel coat, her knitted tea cosy hat, thick tartan tights and brown leather hiking boots.

"Here he is!" Dad exclaims as I sag through the door. "Here's the young man."

Miss Street peers over her little round glasses, looking me up and down. She seems a bit disappointed although I can't think why. "Well, he does seem quite grown up," she says uncertainly.

I place my sports bag temporarily in the empty space where the burglar alarm used to be.

Dad grins at me. "Miss Street's just explained that she's unable to go on the holiday herself," he tells me. "We did wonder if you might want to go."

My heart starts lifting skywards as the picture on the yellow T-shirt zooms back into vision – the deck chair and the palm trees, the parasol and the beach towel. Sun and sea and sand. My lips start creasing into a sudden smile. I stare at Miss Street.

I'm just about to jump up and down and yelp around the swimming pool again when she adds, "I thought you could keep an eye on Mother and Father for me." She motions to her Morris Minor – almost as ancient as her duffel coat – parked beside the Victorian standard lamp.

I peer outside. I can see now that sitting in the car, huddled on the back seat, are two skeletons wearing knitted, woolly hats. Their wrinkled, wizened skulls peer at us through the back window.

I stare at them in horror. They look as if they ought to be setting off for the local cemetery, not setting off on holiday. No wonder she's so anxious to get rid of them. They probably need lifting into wheelchairs and feeding with a teaspoon. They look as if they need a team of nurses to take away with them, not a twelve-year-old boy.

I purse my lips. I don't want to miss an opportunity. I so much want to go on holiday, but I can't possibly go with them. They've probably never been inside an aeroplane; they'd probably both have heart attacks when we accelerate down the runway. They could die of fright on their first encounter with a camel. They wouldn't understand why there weren't bacon and eggs for breakfast. They'd die of sunstroke on the first day.

I shake my head in frustration. No matter how much I want to go away, I can't possibly go with them.

CHAPTER
NINE

The first I see of Grandma is a pair of mini-skirted legs squeezed into snake-skin, high-heeled boots as she stumbles from her taxi. Dad presents her with his arm to lean on and I realize with horror that the top half of her is clothed in a fur coat – a real one.

"Hello, Gran." I give her my best sweet Christmassy smile as I walk down the drive to meet her.

Gran is also wearing a fur hat. She has bright red lipstick and make-up thick enough to cover the cracks in our swimming pool. But not thick enough to camouflage the wrinkles around her mouth and underneath her eyes.

"Here's the young man," says Dad.

I know, of course, exactly what she's going to say, especially as she hasn't seen me since I was seven.

"Well." She stops and stares. But then she doesn't say anything at all. She looks bewildered, as if she can't remember where she is. Or who she is. Or who I am.

I step towards her and Gran places her arms hesitantly round my shoulders, engulfing me in a cloud of perfume strong enough to obliterate Sheffield's ozone layer. She reaches down her face for me to kiss. I take a deep breath, but can't help cringing slightly as my lips make contact with her skin. "Nice to see you, Grandma," I tell her, smiling my smile even sweeter. "Merry Christmas."

"And what do you think of Christmas so far then, George? Is it Praise or Grumble?"

"Well, Bob, it's Praise and Grumble. Praise for the satellite TV and video and for the bowls of nuts and the mince pies. Praise that the central heating's on at last and my bedroom's starting to defrost. And praise for the Christmas tree and the fairy lights."

"But what about the Grumbles, George..?"

I tried not to grumble at first, when we squeezed round the supermarket, stacking our trolley with turkey, chestnut stuffing, cranberry sauce, Christmas pudding and boxes of peanuts and crisps. There were carols on the loudspeaker; there was a giant Christmas tree with fairy lights standing by the oven-ready

67

turkeys; there were streamers across the ceiling and there were shop assistants wearing Father Christmas hats, false beards and rosy red cheeks.

"Here we are, young man." Dad grinned as he handed me a pair of carrier bags. "All the ingredients for a perfect Christmas, eh?"

I nodded and smiled as I picked up the bags.

Just by the exit doors, they have a notice-board crammed with adverts. I paused as I saw a card with:

FRIDGE FOR SALE £20

and another advertising:

COLOUR TV £15

The notice-board was crammed with adverts for videos, microwaves and all the other things we were going to buy from Meadowhall. "Look." I pointed as well as I could with a shopping bag over my arm.

But Dad hardly gave the notice-board a single glance. He doesn't believe in buying second-hand. "Come on," he said. "Let's take this lot home, then we can set off and do the real shopping."

Meadowhall is a huge covered-in shopping centre next to the motorway. It has its own railway station, bus station, cinema and food hall.

When Dad and I arrived, the Salvation Army band were playing Christmas carols. There were inflatable reindeer flying across the entrance and every shop had its own decorations, Christmas tree and fairy lights.

We rose in the gold and glass egg-shaped lift to the upper mall and bustled with the Christmas crowds to choose our new CD mini hi-fi system, our video and our stereo satellite receiver with black mesh dish. We bought a touch-control microwave oven and a fridge-freezer big enough to stand inside. Then we glided down the escalators into the Oasis food hall to choose between the Chocolate Factory, Kentucky Fried Chicken, the Waffle Bar, Singapore Sam's or Burger King. My mouth began to water with the smell of so much food.

I saved some seats at a table next to the fountain while Dad joined the queue at Singapore Sam's. There were more Christmas carols on the loudspeaker as I watched the cartoons on the sixteen-screen vidi-wall and kept telling myself I was happy.

I say kept telling myself because that's what I had to do. Dad had spent more money in the first shop alone than we'd got for the sale of the holiday. All he'd done was to pay a deposit. Everything was signed on hire purchase. In spite of the excitement and the Christmas carols and the cartoons and the wonderful smell of food, I felt something like the golden-egg lift sinking down, down, down through my inside. We were lighting a time bomb.

"Here we are then – sweet and sour chicken, prawn cracklets, egg fried rice, special fruit salad and a milk-shake."

I took my meal on its plastic tray with its plastic knife and fork wrapped in a paper napkin. "Thanks."

I looked up at Dad and smiled.

CHAPTER
TEN

Grandma's idea of a perfect Christmas involves eating chocolates, drinking Tia Maria and watching cartoons on TV.

Zebedee pings over a hedge and lands in front of Ermintrude the cow as I pass Grandma the box of chocolates.

"Another chocolate Brazil, Grandma?"

Grandma looks at me a little strangely. "Time for bed?" she asks.

"No, Gran. Time for a chocolate Brazil. Would you like one?" I jiggle the box in front of her.

Gran stares at the box with a puzzled look, then reaches out and takes it. She pops a chocolate into her mouth and smiles at me. Then she places the box on her lap. Surely, she isn't going to sit there and eat the whole box herself? I haven't had mine yet.

I had expected Gran would want to go on trips. I thought she might like to see the new multi-screen cinema at Meadowhall; I thought we might have all gone there to see a film together, calling at the pick 'n' mix shop. I thought Gran might have wanted to go shopping and ordered a taxi into town, calling at the Blades Souvenir Shop to stock up on Christmas gifts. I have, in fact, got a list of suggestions for those already prepared but Grandma hasn't asked to see it.

She smiles at Ermintrude the cow and pops another chocolate into her mouth.

"Time for bed," she tells me.

Since we installed the satellite dish, we've been studying the *Radio Times* and highlighting our favourite programmes with pink marker pen. Gran, however, sits directly in front of the TV with the remote control buttons clasped firmly in her fist. When we had hopes of getting glued to James Bond, she had her eyes peeled for *Bananaman*. When we were hoping to crown our evening with *Coronation Street*, she was steaming away with *Thomas the Tank Engine*.

We did manage to change the bill from *Dynamo Duck* to *EastEnders* while she was poking bits of popcorn from her teeth. We thought she hadn't noticed, but as soon as Mum went to refill her glass, Gran grabbed the remote control and switched straight back again.

Now it's Christmas Eve and my Christmas present list is still lying upstairs on my desk. Unopened. Gran never asked to see it. She did go to town yesterday, but when I tried to explain about the United souvenir shop, she just said, "Time for bed," and walked straight out of the door.

"Chocolate liqueur?" Mum passes her the box but as soon as Gran has chosen her chocolate, she whisks it away again.

Gran pops the chocolate into her mouth, the liqueur dribbling slightly down her powdered chin. "You shall go to the ball," she exclaims as the Fairy Godmother waves her wand over Cinderella's pumpkin.

Mum refills Gran's glass with Tia Maria.

I turn my gaze to the screen, where Cinderella is climbing into her golden coach with its uniformed footmen and team of white horses. I smile my best Christmas smile.

The fairy lights are winking on the Christmas tree and the room is nice and warm. In between the white plaster cherubs in the corners of the ceiling, there's a

Happy Christmas

in flashing red and white and blue bulbs, garlanded with sprigs of holly. There are chains of Father Christmases pinned around the walls and woven between my strings of recycled milk-bottle tops. The cocktail cabinet

has an assortment of soft drinks – Coke and
ginger ale and lemonade as well as the rapidly
diminishing stock of Tia Maria, sherry,
whisky, gin and Irish Cream.

Gran sucks loudly on her liqueur. "You shall
go to the ball," she slurps at me.

I sit back and try to relax.

Off you go now to the ball.
Dance and be happy –
one and all.

I know I should be proud to have played
the part of fairy godmother, because that's
what I did when I won the holiday, providing
the money for a perfect, proper Christmas.

But before the horses whisk you away,
Heed the words I have to say:

But being only twelve years old, as I've mentioned before, no one ever listens to what I
have to say.

"More Tia Maria?" Dad refills the glasses
and fetches me another Coke.

"Salted cashews, anyone?"

You must be home, Cinderella, my dear,
before the hour of twelve –
or fear…

I can't give out any warnings because nobody wants to listen. And anyway, we can't
be home by twelve o' clock because this is

our home; we don't have anywhere else to go.

...that old rags will replace your
beautiful gown
and your team of white horses will
shrink right down...

There will be no prince hunting the streets for us, carrying the glass slipper on a cushion, begging us to go and live with him in his palace. Our riches will turn back to rags when we miss the first instalment on all the hire purchase agreements.

...to the small white mice they were before
scratching and scurrying over the floor.

The TV and the video, the satellite dish, the fridge-freezer and the microwave – everything will have to go back to the shop.

Grandma grabs a handful of cashew nuts as she watches Cinderella, sparkling in her ballgown, waving from the window of her carriage. "You *shall* go to the ball," she announces, cramming the nuts into her chocolate-filled mouth.

And because my parents are so certain that turning rags into riches is the only way we can be truly happy, they will sit in misery again – once the ball is over – watching through their window, hoping for the day when another fairy godmother will fly past, waving her magic wand.

CHAPTER
ELEVEN

Christmas Day.

The turkey is sizzling in the oven. The drinks are cooling in the fridge and Dad's just lit one of his Christmas Day cigars. I've been helping to make the chestnut stuffing and the brandy sauce for the pudding. We were playing a selection of Christmas favourites on our new CD system, but the sound was drowned by Gran's *Wombles of Wimbledon Common* and a chorus from *Sesame Street*.

"Time to open the presents!" Dad announces.

Gran doesn't look up from the Wombles, bouncing along with their litter bags.

He stands in between Gran and the television, forcing her to look up.

"Is it time for a chocolate Brazil?" she asks.

"No, no. Time to open the presents."

When Gran shows no sign of moving, he

reaches for the Tia Maria. "Can I get you something?"

Gran nods with enthusiasm while Mum sidles in front of the TV and discreetly switches it off.

I begin to undo the wrapping on Grandma's Christmas present. It could be a sweatshirt or a track suit but the parcel's a bit thin for either. It feels more like a T-shirt. Never mind, I can wear it in the summer. I was hoping for a season ticket but I don't think Gran will even know what they are.

I made all my own Christmas presents this year in Craft and Design at school. I made an enamelware bracelet for Mum and a pottery ashtray for Dad. In Home Economics, I made some fancy marzipan sweets for Grandma, which I wrapped up in a nice box. There have been quite a few evenings recently when I've fancied dipping into those myself, but I resisted the temptation.

There seems to be more Sellotape than wrapping paper. I was hoping not to tear the paper so I could use it again next year, but it's impossible to undo the present without ripping the paper to pieces. I just hope Gran managed to find the United shop after all – or at least one of the sports shops in the city centre.

At last, I peel off the happy reindeer wrapping paper and ... I just cannot believe my eyes. I stand and gawp at the packet, open-mouthed.

"You *shall* go to the ball," Gran insists.

I swallow hard. There in my outstretched hand is a T-shirt. It's a football shirt but it isn't red and white. Nor is it the United away-strip. It has blue and white stripes and a smiling black and yellow owl perched upon the pocket.

I stare at it open-mouthed.

I become aware of the embarrassed glances exchanged between my parents. Mum is nodding and smiling, willing me to say I like the shirt, willing me to tell Grandma that it's exactly what I wanted.

"It's a Wednesday shirt."

Everyone nods. There is no denying that it is a Sheffield Wednesday shirt, a football shirt from the club I hate most in all the world.

There's a long pause. I look up at the trio of eager, Christmassy faces.

"Well," Mum says with empty jollity. "It's all football, isn't it?"

I don't say or do anything. I just stare at the shirt, the hard knot returning to my stomach.

"Another Tia Maria, Grandma?" Dad reaches for her glass.

I just can't believe it. *All football.* As if one team is exactly the same as another. As if a Unitedite is just the same as a Wednesdayite. As if there's no such thing as loyalty.

The knot in my stomach tightens like a fist.

"Another Coke, young man?"

Mum slides towards me while Gran's attention is distracted. "It wouldn't hurt you to wear it," she tells me in a low voice, "just while your grandma's here."

And it is this last remark which is, quite suddenly, the very last straw. Wouldn't hurt me to wear it????!!!!

Suddenly, quite suddenly, I have had enough. The taut fist in my stomach flexes and I feel a very strong desire to tear the T-shirt into shreds. I look up at the Christmas tree with its twinkling lights, and suddenly I want to kick down the tree and smash it through the window. I could tear up the fairy lights and the rows of Father Christmases. And if Grandma tells me I can go to the ball again, I shall be very tempted to knock her Tia Maria flying and tip the bottle all over her head.

Because suddenly I have had enough of my let's-pretend-we're-having-an-ever-such-a-jolly-Christmas family. Enough of my drunken, divvy granny and her dribbling chocolates. Enough of a family who feed me on bread and dripping, who give me a freezing cold bedroom to sleep in and leave me alone to fend off burglars while they swan off to the pub. I have had enough of missing every football match so far of the season.

I have tried very, very hard. I have tried hard to be patient. I have tried hard to keep quiet. I have tried to be loyal to my family, backing

79

them through thick and thin. And now, quite suddenly, I feel as though I'm playing for the wrong team at the opposite end of the ground. I can hear a distant whistle blowing somewhere, telling me it's time to stop the game and leave the pitch.

It's all football, isn't it?

Well, no, it bloody isn't. I will not be seen dead in a Sheffield Wednesday T-shirt. I would rather be fried in oil than wear a Sheffield Wednesday T-shirt. Even in the privacy of my own home,where no one else can see me. Even in bed. Even sitting on the bog. I will not wear a Sheffield Wednesday T-shirt. Not even to be sick in. Not any time and not for anyone.

There is such a thing as loyalty.

And I am loyal to my team.

I am a true United fan.

For ever.

─ HALF-TIME ─

THE
SECOND HALF

CHAPTER
TWELVE

"Well, good morning, everybody. I hope you all had a good flight. My name's Gayle. I'm your tour representative and I'd like to begin by welcoming you to the beautiful island of Djerba."

I rub my eyes against the sunlight streaming through the window. I can hardly believe that I'm here. This is not a dream, I keep telling myself. I have arrrived in Djerba all on my own.

I've made it.

I pick up my free drink of tropical fruit juice, then sit on the large settee next to Kelly and her mum. I'm pleased I got talking to people on the plane and made some friends; otherwise I'd be feeling a bit lost.

This time yesterday, I was packing my suitcase, checking my passport and waiting for Miss Street to collect me on her way to Manchester Airport. I didn't dare believe I was really going on holiday until I climbed up the steps of the plane.

"Now, I'm going to give you some information about the hotel and places to visit, so if you've got a pen and paper..."

My pockets contain a couple of hard-boiled eggs, some breadcakes, date jam and yogurt, but no pen.

Kelly's mum passes me a Biro.

At first, the idea seemed totally ridiculous. I never really believed that Mum and Dad would let me come here on my own. Then I thought my passport would be out of date. Then I thought that Miss Street would have found someone else to keep an eye on her parents – or Grumps and Gramps, as she asked me to call them.

"First of all, the meal times: the breakfast buffet is served from half past seven. You can choose whatever you like and go back as often as you want."

That's why my pockets are filled with hard-boiled eggs. I've saved them for Mr and Mrs Street, who don't seem to have found their way yet to the dining hall.

"Evening meal starts at seven, and again, you can help yourself and eat as much as you like."

My mouth waters with the prospect of

eating as much as I want, every day for two whole weeks, but Kelly raises her hand. "What about lunch?" she asks.

"Well, there are lots of cafés around the complex and in the town," Gayle explains. "You can buy pizzas and sandwiches..."

I haven't brought much money. It looks as though I might need the boiled eggs after all.

"Now, the sports facilities..."

In the end, everything turned out all right.

My passport was still in order from the skiing trip I went on with my private school. Dad sat me down and gave me a long lecture on the dangers of talking to strange men, taking drugs, getting sunburnt, drinking unsafe water and getting a dodgy tummy. But then, to my amazement, he told me that – if I promised not to stray too far from the hotel – I could go.

The most surprising thing was that Cherry Street still hadn't found anyone to take the extra ticket. "I have had several offers from people," she told us, "but for some reason, as soon as I introduced them to Grumps and Gramps, they seemed to change their minds."

I make notes about the swimming pool and cycle hire, the disco and the tennis but I find it hard to take it all in. We didn't arrive until 3 a.m. and I haven't had much sleep. All I really want to do is go down and laze on the beach.

"Have you seen Grumps and Gramps?" Kelly's mum whispers.

I shake my head.

"We'd better go and look for them," she suggests, "as soon as the talk's finished."

Grumps and Gramps have been the only problem. At meal time on the plane, I had to stop them emptying their sugar sachets into their egg mayonnaise, which they'd both mistaken for custard. When we landed, I had to chase after their trolley, piled up high with luggage, after they sent it careering down towards the main runway. Then, when we lost them both in Djerba Airport, I had to fish them out of the departure lounge, where I found them in the queue for the first flight to Islamabad. Now I haven't seen them since last night.

Gayle outlines the trips we can go on but most of them are much too expensive for me. And I hardly think Grumps and Gramps will want to spend three nights sleeping in Bedouin tents in the desert or go on a camel train to the oasis.

I glance out of the window at the sunshine and the palm trees and think of the slushy snow I left behind in Sheffield.

"I think I'll just nip down to the beach," I tell Kelly and her mum. "Shall I meet you later?"

"Well, we were thinking of taking a

pedalo," says Kelly. "Shall we meet you in the café on the beach?"

Walking down the path towards the sea, I have to keep screwing my eyes against the sun – a sun brighter and even more yellow than the Sheffield United T-shirt which I'm wearing at last.

It was the T-shirt that made me decide. Standing in my room on Christmas Day, my face burning red with anger, I stared at the two shirts lying on my bed. One was the hated, blue Wednesday stripes with their fat owl perched upon the pocket. The other was my yellow United shirt with the palm tree and the deck-chair. There was no doubt at all which one I wanted to wear.

And then, of course, I remembered Grumps and Gramps. I remembered seeing them sitting in the back of Cherry's car. I remembered how she wanted someone to look after them on holiday. Surely spending two weeks nursing a wizened pair of skeletons must be better than being forced to wear a Sheffield Wednesday shirt on Christmas Day?

I thread my way along the little paths in between the white-domed chalets. There isn't any grass. Instead there are plants like cacti – prickly and squidgy – sprouting from the sand. There are no ordinary trees, only tall palms with bunches of dates hanging down.

My dad found the piece of paper with Cherry Street's name and phone number. "Well," he said when I asked him about the holiday, "she'll probably have found someone else by now, but it won't do any harm to ask."

So, here I am.

I emerge from the rows of chalets, then stop and stare at the sea. Deep, brilliant dark blue, flat as a field with white crests rippling against the silver sand.

This is what I came here for.

I sit down on an empty sunbed under a beach umbrella and gaze towards the horizon. The sky is a deep dark blue without a single cloud. The sun is hot already and it's only halfway through the morning.

Mum and Dad and Gran will be scraping the last few bones off the turkey as their day is enveloped by *Postman Pat* or littered with choruses of Wombles. Mum will get more and more grumpy as Gran drains the bottles in the cocktail cabinet. Dad will begin his phone calls, making up excuses to stave off the first payments on all our Christmas purchases. And all I had to do was turn around and walk off the end of the pitch.

Of course, I feel nervous because I've never been on holiday on my own before. I'm not intending to take drugs or talk to strange men, but I'm sure those aren't the only potential hazards.

I take off my shoes and socks and put my feet up on the sunbed.

The important thing is, I tell myself, that I'm here now. I've made friends already and the only real problem is that I've no idea what's happened to Grumps and Gramps.

CHAPTER THIRTEEN

"Hello. You Engleesh, yes?"

I'm not sure where I am at first. I open my eyes, then cover them to ward off an explosion of glaring red and yellow circles. There's a strange warm smell, almost a farmyard smell, and a nearby asthmatic wheezing.

"You like Djerba?"

I part my fingers and allow my eyes to focus on the hem of a long, striped, multicoloured garment. I look up to see a smiling Arab with very dark skin and a long white headdress.

"Yes, yes, thank you. It's very nice."

"Me, Mohammed. How do you do?"

"Hello. How do you do."

I'm aware of Dad's warning about talking to strange men but it does seem rude to walk away. Also, there's a shuffling round my sunbed, something warm and steamy down my back. I glance hesitantly over my shoulder, then suddenly I almost leap straight into the air. Nuzzling round my armpit is a large, shaggy· carpet, breathing steam into my left ear.

"You like ride?"

I used to enjoy the occasional donkey ride and I'm normally fairly fond of animals, but ...

"You ride camel?"

... this creature doesn't look as sweet-tempered as a donkey. It's kneeling beside me with its bony knees resting on the sand and it's trying to eat my T-shirt.

I smile and shake my head as politely as I can while springing to my feet and sprinting down the beach. "Well, that's very kind of you," I call to Mohammed, "but I, er..." I leave the sunbed and the camel far behind and head towards the café.

Fortunately, I don't seem to have slept for long and I can see Kelly and her mum still waiting for me on the terrace.

I scour the groups of sunbathers as I run past, searching for Grumps and Gramps. Many of the ladies, however, are lying topless and when I stare at them, I begin to get some funny looks. I've got a feeling, anyhow, that Gramps won't have removed so many of her clothes. The last time I saw her, she was wearing hiking boots, woolly socks, a long skirt and jumper and a winter coat.

Kelly and her mum are sizzling in the sunshine with a jug of tropical fruit juice, lots of ice and an extra glass for me. "Have you found Grumps and Gramps yet?" asks Kelly.

The fruit juice is just what I need to help restore my energy and Kelly's mum is considerate enough to order another jugful.

"No. I still haven't seen them since last night."

"Don't you know their room number?"

I shake my head. "The porter took me to my room first. By the time I'd unlocked my door and put my cases down, they'd vanished."

"We'll have to ask Reception for their room number," says Kelly's mum. "Perhaps you'd better wait until later, for the pedalo ride."

As the three of us walk back along the beach, we see an odd-looking couple sitting with their sunbeds fastened upright as straight as dining chairs. The man is wearing a brown suit, waistcoat, white shirt, tie and a trilby hat and is leaning on a walking-stick. The woman wears a raincoat, thick stockings and hiking boots and has a large shopping bag over her arm.

So this is where they are.

Grumps and Gramps look as out of place on a holiday beach as my Sheffield Wednesday shirt would on the Kop at Bramall Lane.

"Hello, there!" I shout.

They turn their heads towards us but show no sign of recognition.

"We wondered where you'd got to."

It has to be them; they're wearing the same clothes they were wearing at the airport. Surely, they can't have forgotten who we all are?

"It's me. George."

Grumps stares up at me quizzically.

"Don't you remember me? And Kelly? And Kelly's mum?"

Gramps takes out her glasses and peers through them.

"Is it the man with the camel?" Grumps asks her.

"No," she says, "it's that boy we met at the airport."

"Airport?" asks Grumps. "What airport?"

I try not to look at Kelly, who's shaking her head in dismay. Instead, I take the boiled eggs from my pocket. "I've brought you some breakfast." I take out the bread rolls – a bit squashed now – and the yogurt. "I didn't see you in the dining-room."

"He was standing in the airport," Gramps recollects. "He helped us with the cases."

I nod. "I'm George."

Grumps stares at me incredulously. "By George!" he exclaims. "How did you get here?"

How does he think I got here?

Does he imagine that I cycled over on a

pedalo? Floated on an airbed? Dropped down in a parachute?

I sigh deeply. "I flew," I tell him.

We take Grumps and Gramps for a stroll along the seafront. "Well, it's a grand day," says Grumps as he pauses every couple of minutes to get his breath.

I try walking in slow motion, lifting my legs as if they're embedded in quick-drying concrete. Kelly and her mum keep bending down and collecting shells, but we still have to stand and wait every few metres for Grumps and Gramps to catch up.

We arrive, with much relief, at a cluster of ramshackle tables and chairs. "Well, I'm ready for a sit-down," says Gramps.

There's a tumbledown shack made of palm leaves with a cardboard sign:

THE HAPPY CAMEL
Snack Bar And Café

and a couple of sad-looking camels kneeling on the sand. A nanny goat and a family of baby kids nibble at scraps of cactus in between the tables.

"Well, I just fancy a nice pot of tea," says Gramps. "I wonder if we could get a toasted teacake."

We sit down.

An elderly Arab hobbles by, leading a donkey whose baskets are piled high with bananas and dates. Grumps waves his walking-stick at him. "It's a grand day," he tells him.

The donkey man nods and smiles and waves a banana at us. A young man wearing jeans and Arabian scarf emerges from the little shack. "Engleesh?"

"That's right," Gramps tells him. "We normally go to Skegness."

The young man shakes hands vigorously. "Hello, Mr Skegness. Welcome to Happy Camel. Me..." he points to himself "...Assid."

"Well, thank you very much, Sid," says Grumps. "Now, we'd like a pot of tea for three. And we did wonder about some toasted teacakes..."

Assid doesn't have any teacakes but he makes us a tray of tea and bread and butter. Grumps looks at me uncertainly as he pours a cup of tea. "Have we met you before at all?" he asks.

"I'm George."

"He looks a bit like that boy we met at the coach station," says Gramps.

"What coach station?"

"You know, when the luggage trolley ran away."

Kelly and I exchange glances, but Kelly's mum signals with her finger on her lips.

"Have you been staying here long?" asks Gramps.

"I arrived last night," I explain, patting one of the goats nosing underneath the table. "I came from Sheffield."

"Well, would you believe it?" says Grumps. "It's a small world, isn't it, eh?"

"Well, just fancy," says Gramps. She turns to Kelly's mum. "We come from Sheffield as well, you know. Well, it is a small world, isn't it, eh? What a coincidence."

Kelly tries not to giggle as I pass her the bread and butter.

Assid re-emerges from his shack. "Please?" He points to a chair.

We all nod and smile and he joins us at our table.

"Well, it's a grand day," announces Grumps, stirring his tea.

"We haven't been here before," Gramps explains. "We normally go to Skegness. We stay at Mrs Basset's boarding-house."

"I like to go fishing. *Fishing*." Grumps mimes the throwing and winding of a fishing-rod and suddenly Assid's face lights up.

"You like fish?"

Grumps nods. "Fish." He makes swimming

motions with his arm. "*Fish*. That's right."

Assid points towards the sea, where two rods are standing by the water's edge. "Come. I show you." He helps Grumps to his feet and leads him to the fishing-rods.

The rest of us drink our tea.

"Mrs Basset's boarding-house," Gramps explains, "is just down by the pier. I don't know if you know it at all…"

We all shake our heads.

"But the weather's not like this. It's very bracing in Skegness."

"Well, it's a lovely day today," says Kelly's mum.

"We normally go with our Cherry," Gramps carries on. "But she's got a boyfriend now."

Boyfriend? She looked old enough for great-grandchildren and a zimmer frame. But not for boyfriends.

"She wanted a week with him."

Grumps turns suddenly towards us, his eyes glowing brightly. "Fish 'n' chips all round, eh?" he shouts. "How about that? Out of the sea, straight on to the cooker." He points to a small barbecue placed next to the fishing-rods. "We won't get fish fresher than that, eh?"

He hobbles back up the beach as Assid goes to light the barbecue. "Well, you should just see that," he tells us. "Yon lad gets up first thing in the morning, collects his lugworms, then catches all his fish before the customers come in. You should just see the size of that there fishing-rod."

He sits back down at the table. "We go out on a fishing boat at Skeggy," he tells me. "*Rover's Return*. You only need a short rod for that." He nods with admiration at Assid's morning catch. "Now that's what I call proper fishing, that is."

CHAPTER FOURTEEN

"You do know how to sail one of these things, don't you?"

I've never actually been on a pedalo before but I can ride a bike and it seems a similar idea. It's a kind of two-person bicycle-on-water. "Oh, they're really easy," I say to Kelly, keeping my fingers crossed.

Bloated with the best meal I've eaten in years, I haul myself into the boat. If I'd eaten one more spoonful, I'd be turning the pedalo into a submarine.

"Don't go too far out," the boatman tells us. "The next stop's Libya."

Kelly and I both soak our feet as we clamber into the boat. Then we rock perilously from side to side when the boatman shoves us out to sea, but after that it seems quite easy. The sea is very calm and all we have to do is steer and pedal.

"What's wrong with going to Libya?" I ask.

"It's one of those countries where they chop people's hands off for stealing a few biscuits. Things like that."

I think of the boiled eggs from breakfast still stored in my pocket for emergency supplies. They could well be stamped with the name of the hotel, like the towels in my chalet. "Well, perhaps we'd better not go too far," I suggest.

Kelly and I pedal past the swimmers and the windsurfers. We manage not to bump into the rocks. We wave and shout hello to all the other pedalos we pass. The sea is a clear, cool blue and we can see small shoals of fish scuttling along beside us.

"Do you think Grumps and Gramps will be all right?" asks Kelly.

"They seemed all right when we left them."

Our fantastic meal of barbecued fish had been followed by cheese, dates, ice-cream and litres of drinks.

Assid and Grumps talked about shallow fishing, deep sea fishing, fishing-rods and lugworms. Gramps and Kelly's mum talked about Cherry and her new boyfriend. Kelly and I just ordered more ice-cream and tropical fruit juice and Grumps insisted on paying the bill.

"Well, it's a grand day!" shouts Kelly, waving an imaginary walking-stick at a large seagull. "Have I met you before somewhere? What did you say your name was? By George!" she turns to me with a look of mock amazement. "That there seagull's come all the way from Sheffield. By gum! It's a small world!"

I wish Kelly wouldn't make me laugh because every time I chuckle, the pedalo rocks backwards and forwards and we finish up spinning round in circles.

"And now it's over to young George, out there on the Isle of Djerba. And what do you think of the holiday so far, George? Is is Praise or Grumble?"

"Well, it's Praise and Grumble, Bob. Praise for the holiday because really, things couldn't be better. I've made some very good friends already. I've got a wonderful chalet all to myself with my own bathroom, right next to the beach. The hotel is very good, with lots of facilities and the weather here is glorious."

"And what about the Grumbles, George?"

"Well, of course, there's not much in the way of football, though I can manage without that for two weeks. But there's Grumps and Gramps. I mean, I don't think they should really have come away by themselves. Most of the time, they don't seem to know where they are, or even who they are..."

*   *   *

When I arrive at Grumps and Gramps' chalet to take them for their evening meal, I find everywhere in darkness. I know I've got the right number because I've been to check at Reception. I assume that, like me, they must have fallen asleep, so I tap gently on the window. When there's no reply, I shout, "Anybody there? George here."

But there's no answer.

I leave the chalet and wander towards the beach. It's getting dark now; the sunbeds have been stacked together and the parasols lie folded in a heap.

I don't know what to do. I don't want to go and have my dinner until I've found Grumps and Gramps but, of course, they might have found their own way to the dining-room.

I set off towards The Kalif. Even though I ate such a big lunch, my mouth starts watering and my nostrils quiver with the distant smell of soup.

I stand inside the door of the dining-room. Waiters bustle over to try and find me somewhere to sit, but I shake my head as I inspect the tables one at a time. There are several people I recognize from this morning, but now they have sunburnt noses, red cheeks or burnt bald patches on top of their heads.

The tomato soup smells delicious and I

notice that there's a choice of roast chicken, lasagne or lamb chops.

"All right, George?"

"I've lost Grumps and Gramps again," I explain to Kelly's mum.

"Oh, not again!" moans Kelly.

"Shall we have a look outside?"

We walk back out and gaze along the empty shopping precinct, past the shuttered gift shops and the cafés. And then I see the camel, plodding past the pizza parlour. It's being led along by Mohammed, the man I met on the beach.

As the camel approaches, I can see two figures sitting on its back. There's an old woman with a long knitted cardigan, thick stockings and hiking boots; there's an old man wearing a brown suit and trilby hat. "There they are!" I shout."

"No!" says Kelly's mum. "Surely not. They won't be riding on a camel."

"Yes, they are."

"He's right," says Kelly.

"Well, who'd have thought it?"

The camel rounds the corner and plods past the disco.

"Hooray!" we all shout, as Grumps waves his walking-stick in the air.

"By George!" he shouts. "It's been a grand day."

* * *

Dear Mum & Dad & Gram,

   Got here all right. Having
a smashing time. Very sunny.

   Grumps and Gramps have
been riding on a camel.

   Made a new friend called
Kelly.

   Happy New Year!

                 Love,
                 George
                 × × × ×

CHAPTER
FIFTEEN

On Day 2, I discover that I can contact Grumps and Gramps by phoning the number of their chalet.

"Hello, there. George here."

"Is that the man with the camel?"

"No, no. George. Don't you remember me? From Sheffield."

"Well, what a coincidence! Hey, there's a lad here says he's from Sheffield. Well, I'll be jiggered. Hey, it's a small world."

"I was with you yesterday. Don't you remember me?"

"No. No, we haven't ordered any tea. We were just thinkin' of havin' some breakfast."

"Listen, I'll be round at your chalet in ten minutes. I'll take you along to the dining-room."

"All right, then. Will you be bringin' that there camel?"

After a bit of a struggle, I manage to show Grumps and Gramps how to pick up their trays and collect boiled eggs, hot bread rolls, date jam and butter. Then I demonstrate how to obtain tea and orange juice by turning the taps on the drinks dispensers.

They both manage to squirt tea and orange juice over their boiled eggs, over the toast and down the legs of a queue of French and German guests. "Oh dear," says Grumps, "did I dribble down your sock? Well, it's a grand day again. We've been for a ride on a camel, you know."

Grumps has now left his jacket and hat behind, but still wears his collar and tie, red braces and knitted waistcoat. Gramps is wearing a long flowered dress with her woolly cardi over the top and she's carrying her shopping bag and a very large sun hat. They speak broad Yorkshire to everyone they meet – English, French, Arabs and Germans. When no one understands them, Grumps draws pictures with his walking-stick.

"We've found a grand café," Gramps tells Otto and Lotto, the German couple sitting at our breakfast table. "They serve fish straight out of the sea."

When they don't seem to understand, Grumps draws a picture of a camel in the air with his walking-stick. Then he mimes picking up a knife and fork and eating a big meal. Otto and Lotto don't look very enthusiastic.

"German people no like camel for dinner," Otto explains. "We go for happy pizza."

After breakfast, I decide to take a swim. "I'll call for you later," I explain to Gramps. "Shall we go back to The Happy Camel?"

"We've found this really good café," Gramps is now explaining to the French couple who've just arrived.

"This lad," says Grumps, "has a fishing-rod twice as tall as I am and he does it all with lugworms."

"I'll see you later." I wave goodbye and go to collect my trunks.

The weather is just right for a morning swim. The sun, of course, is shining, the sky is a clear, deep blue and the water is cool and refreshing. The poolside bar echoes with the shaking of cocktails and tinkle of ice. Arabian music crackles out of the loudspeakers.

I swim a length, then float on my back with the cool water rippling round my chin. Then I sit on the edge of the pool and watch the dates ripening on the palm tree. As the sun starts getting hotter, I slide back in the water and crawl for two more lengths, but after that, I'm ready for a rest.

I climb out of the pool and rub myself down

with a towel. Then I pull on my jeans and set off for the beach.

The sand is speckled with sunbeds and sun-bathers. People are paddling, swimming, eating ice-creams and reading foreign newspapers. I can't see Grumps and Gramps.

I walk instead to the water's edge, where a small crowd is gazing out to sea. They're viewing an incident involving a fishing boat, a fishing line, a sunhat, a walking-stick and a pedalo.

Grumps and Gramps are sitting in the pedalo out at sea. Somehow, they've managed to become entangled with the line of a nearby fishing boat. Grumps is pedalling as hard as he can, but seems to have no idea how to steer the pedalo, which goes round and round in circles, tying them up like a maypole.

Gramps' sunhat has blown off and Grumps keeps reaching over to try and hook it with his walking-stick. Meanwhile, the fisherman is struggling to haul in a huge fish which keeps bobbing up and down on the fishing-line against the side of the pedalo.

Lotto, the German woman, is standing on the beach. "Catch the fish!" she calls out to Grumps.

"Grab the hat!" yells Otto.

Grumps reaches over once more and there's a loud "Oooooohh!" from the crowd as the pedalo tips.

Of course, Grumps and Gramps haven't gone far out to sea and the water isn't very deep but I don't think Grumps would be able to swim very easily – not in his shirt and tie, braces and woolly cardigan.

The hooked fish flies across the pedalo once more. Gramps makes a brave attempt to catch it in her shopping bag.

"Oohhhh!" groans the crowd as the fish slithers back.

"Oooooooh!!" they shout when the pedalo keels as Gramps tries to regain her balance.

I'm already wearing my swimming trunks so I only need to take off my trainers and jeans and peel off my T-shirt. I pile my clothes on the beach, then take a deep breath and run straight into the water.

The sea is much colder than the pool. My first reaction, as the waves bite, is to turn around and run straight out again. I glance ahead, however, at the rocking pedalo and force myself to run faster, splashing through the waves.

The cold water lashes at my legs, making me gasp out loud. The shore shelves very gently so I can wade up to my chest and then my armpits. But the pedalo is further than I realized. I have to throw myself forward and start to swim.

I swallow mouthfuls of salty water as the waves rise over my chin, but it doesn't take long to reach the sunhat. I snatch it out of the water, but as I need both my hands for swimming, I have to carry it on my head.

"Hooray!" There's a loud cheer behind me as the hat is rescued.

I swim towards the pedalo, careful not to become entangled in the fishing-line. I place my hands on the boards and, with a bit of help from Grumps' walking-stick, I lever myself on board.

"Hooray!" the crowd roars again.

I stagger to my feet. Of course, I can't help showing off. I stand on the back of the boat, facing the shore, then I sweep off the sunhat and bow graciously to the crowd.

There's a burst of applause. "More!" they shout. "More!" Then, "Watch out for the fish!"

I turn round a second too late. Something cold and wet and clammy is wiggling around my kneecaps. I look down and see the slimy scales, flapping round my legs.

"Oh!" I step backwards. Of course, my legs forget that they're on a boat, so they step on thin air. Next thing I know, I'm toppling backwards and my legs step on to the sea. Then splash! I'm underwater – down, down, down.

The salty water clogs my nose and clouds my eyes. As my feet touch the bottom, I make a massive effort and shoot myself back to the surface. Up, up, up, I emerge, gasping for air.

I reach out to save myself, grabbing the side of the pedalo and almost pull it over.

There's another shout from the shore. "Grab the walking-stick!"

I take a deep breath.

I shake the water from my face and see Grumps, hanging over the edge, pushing his walking-stick towards me. Gramps is leaning over as well, offering her shopping bag. If I grab hold of them both, the boat will probably tip over.

I manage to tread water and, as I do, the fish reappears beside me, dangling on its nylon line. I stare for a couple of seconds at its large, round eyes. Then suddenly, I open the shopping bag, scoop up the flapping, slithery fish and plop it inside.

"He's caught the fish!" shouts Grumps, waving his walking-stick.

"Hooray!" A big cheer from the crowd.

"Hooray!" Another cheer from the fishing crew.

I work my way, hand over hand, to recapture Gramps' sunhat, bobbing on the waves. I place it back on my head. Then I place my hands evenly on both sides of the pedalo and lever myself out of the water.

I fall flat on my face, but it doesn't really matter. I don't capsize the pedalo and I find, with relief, that the fish is being handed over, zipped up in the shopping bag.

CHAPTER SIXTEEN

Two hours later, and we're finishing our lunch in The Happy Camel with cups of coffee and marzipan dates. Grumps and Gramps have recounted the story of their pedalo adventures to everyone in the café.

"We went for a ride on a piccolo," Gramps explains to Kelly's mum. "We were bombarded by a giant fish but George, here, caught it in my shopping bag."

"And he rescued your sunhat," adds Grumps.

Throughout the meal, we're recognized by various people who were watching from the beach. They walk across and shake my hand. "The boy who caught the giant fish!" they announce. And, "The young man in the sunhat."

People stay for coffee, fruit juice, wine or

beer. Some order the freshly barbecued fish. The Happy Camel becomes busier and busier. People offer to buy me drinks and ice-creams. They ask Grumps and Gramps to join them for a glass of wine. The conversation gets louder.

"Look over there," says Gramps. "It's the man with the camel. Yoo-hoo! Mohammed!" she shouts.

"Hello, Mrs Gramps." Mohammed waves his camel-lead at our table. "It's a grand day."

"It certainly is," Grumps tells him. "We've just been tied up on a piccolo."

Mohammed parks his camel next to another one on the beach, then ambles into Assid's shack. He returns with a large, glass hubble-bubble pipe which he sets out on the sand. He sits on a low stool in front of it, lights it up and begins to inhale through a long, snake-like tube.

I feed scraps of food to one of the baby goats hiding underneath the table, and it's at that point, when I look up, that I suddenly see the football.

In front of the café is a line where the tide has gone out, leaving plastic bottles, bits of driftwood and palm leaves. The football is peeping through a pile of rubbish.

I heave myself up from the table, walk across and pick up the football. To my surprise, it seems quite new and clean. I bounce it up and down as I walk back to my table. I throw it to Kelly, who catches it and throws it back. I throw it to Grumps and that's when the idea of the football match is launched.

"Hey," he says, tossing the ball in the air. "We've enough here for two teams, haven't we? Five-a-side."

I nod. Kelly nods. Otto and Lotto both nod. The others look a bit confused.

"Football." I point to the ball and mime kicking it. Then Assid and Mohammed and the donkey man all nod and grin.

Otto stands up and begins to count people in. "One, two, three... What about the goal-posts?" he asks.

I look around. On one side of the beach are two palm trees, just about the right distance apart. "The palm trees can be one goal," I tell him.

"An' them there camels," says Grumps. "So long as they're not thinkin' of going anywhere." Grumps raises himself with diffi-culty out of his seat. "Right then, you lot can be Sheffield Wednesday and us lot'll be United."

"Yes!" shouts Assid. "Manchester United."

"No, no, no, lad," Grumps corrects him. "Not Manchester United – *Sheffield* United."

I nod approvingly.

"Sheffield United. The Blades. Now listen... La da da daaa." Grumps gives them the tune to "We Are Sailing" as he instructs the players facing the palm trees:

We are Blades men, super Blades men
we are Blades men, from the Lane...

Some of them start singing "soup for Blades men" and "from the rain", but they manage the tune all right.

Sheffield Wednesday have a bit more trouble. I manage to translate the word Wednesday into French and Kelly translates it into German but it only causes more confusion. Kelly teaches them the chant:

Wednesday! Wednesday! Wednesday!

"I play goal," offers Mohammed and he strolls across to sit between the palm trees, taking his hubble-bubble with him. He has, of course, quite sensibly, chosen the only bit of shade on the beach.

"Now, who wants to be Callum Welly?" asks Grumps.

I'm not much good at football. I'm a spectator, not a player. When we have a knockabout at school, I offer to play in goal because you don't have to move around as much. And it is a very hot day. And I've eaten a very big lunch.

"That's me," I offer, then position myself in between the two camels. One of them opens one eye and stares at me but the other shows very little interest.

"Now, who wants to be Mitch Waddle?"

The Wednesday players look round in confusion.

Gramps tries to impersonate a duck, quacking and waddling her shopping bag up and down the pitch, but it doesn't make things any clearer.

"I be striker," offers Otto.

"That's all right, then," Kelly explains. "Waddle's the striker for Wednesday."

"I be Paul Gascoigne," offers Assid.

"No, no, no, lad," Grumps corrects him. "You're a United man now. You can be John Little."

And so, we get organized. Playing for United, we have Grumps and Assid as the two strikers, Kelly and her mum in midfield and myself in goal.

You fill up my senses
like a gallon of Magnet
like a packet of Woodbines
like a good pinch of snuff.
Like a night out in **Sheffield**
like a greasy chip butty,
come, Sheffield United,
come fill me again.
La da da de … ooo!

The Wednesday team consists of Otto and the donkey man on the front line, Gramps and Lotto playing midfield and Mohammed in goal.

And off we go.

The first goal is scored, much to my embarrassment, within the first few seconds. Otto, the German Mitch Waddle, is rather large. He isn't young, but he's not as old as Grumps and Gramps, and has a body like a tank. He takes the ball, then strolls down with it towards the goal. I wait for Kelly or her mum to tackle, but both stand waiting for each other as he dribbles the ball straight through. I stand and wait.

> *Goo-on-den!*
> *Goo-on-den!*
> *Goo-on-den!*

shout the supporters, gathered on the edge of the pitch. Otto takes aim, and the next thing I know, I'm lying flattened on the ground, knocked over by the ball.

> *One-nil. One-nil.*
> *One-nil. One-nil.*
> *One-nil. One-nil.*
> *One-nil. One-nil…*

I stagger back to my feet.

This time, Assid – playing John Little – is ready and waiting. He takes possession and charges across to the right wing, where Gramps is busy, fastening up her cardi. "Just a minute," she tells him, "I'm not ready."

But Assid has already passed her.

Come on, you Blades!

He sidesteps around Grumps and is heading towards the goal when suddenly we have a pitch invasion. The nanny goat and her four kids trot across the sand. Assid trips over them. He kicks the ball as he falls, but Grumps is nowhere near, and it's seized by Otto, who begins his determined stride down towards me and my camels.

This time, our midfield is ready for action.

Come on, you Blades!

Kelly's mum dashes across for the challenge. Otto stands with his legs apart, wondering what to do. Meanwhile, Kelly sneaks behind him, bends down and toes the ball out from in between his legs. Before Otto has time to notice, she's whisked the ball away and passed to Assid, who's now on his feet, clearing goats off the pitch.

And it's Sheffield United,
Sheffield United F.C.
are by far the greatest team
the world has ever seen...

Assid takes delivery but is intercepted by Gramps. There's a bit of toing and froing and a definite foul from the shopping bag, but

Assid recovers the ball.

> *Goo-on-den!*
> *Goo-on-den...*

He stands in front of the palm trees and shoots.

> *Goo-on-den!*
> *Goo-on-den...*

Mohammed, reluctantly, leaves his hookah pipe and begins to rise to his feet, but too late. United have equalized.

> *Y-e-e-e-e-ssss!*
> *David Basset's red and white army!*
> *David Basset's red and white army!*
> *United!*
> *United!*
> *United!*

chant the spectators, which does, after all, sound better than "soup for Blades men".

So, it's back to the centre.

Assid gets the ball.

> *Goo-on-den!*
> *Goo-on-den...*

He passes to Grumps out on the left wing. Grumps stops the ball with his walking-stick, then raises the stick above his shoulder and swipes the ball down towards the goal.

"Foul!" shout the Wednesdayites.

"Hey! This fussball, no cricket," shouts

Mitch Waddle.

The donkey man rushes forward and grabs the ball but is tackled straightaway by Lotto. "He's on your side!" everyone shouts, but Lotto takes no notice. She dribbles the ball down the left wing, skips around Grumps, leaps across his walking-stick and, to my amazement, takes a sudden shot at goal.

Of course, I'm completely unprepared, although, unlike the Wednesday keeper, I am at least on my feet. I spring forward but the ball flies straight through my hands. Fortunately, at that moment, one of the camels decides to shift its position and move its head. In doing so, it hits the ball back into play.

Y-e-e-e-e-ssss!
Na na na na,
He's a Blade. He's a Blade!

shout the Unitedites.

"Foul! That should have been in!" shout the Wednesdayites.

"Rebounded off the goalpost!" Kelly insists.

Shortly after this, there follows my moment of glory. Grumps has to leave the pitch to go and spend a penny. That leaves us one man short. "Can you cover down the wing," he asks me, "while I 'ave a Jimmy Riddle? I'll just nip off and find a bush."

Grumps doesn't seem to have noticed that we're playing in the desert and, apart from the

Wednesday goalposts, there aren't any trees or bushes within sight.

Grumps hobbles off into the distance. Realizing that he's likely to be gone for quite some time, I step out of my camel box and walk forward on a line with Kelly's mum. Kelly has successfully challenged Gramps and is trying to pass across when she's intercepted by Mitch Waddle. Waddle begins his slow run towards the goal. Although he's big, Otto isn't very fit and he's already puffing and panting and turning red in the face. It seems a good time to tackle.

Come on, you Blades!

I move straight in and, to my amazement, take the ball. I head down towards the palm trees, where Lotto, Gramps and the donkey man are discussing whether to order tea or coffee with cakes at half-time. Mohammed, however, has seen me coming.

Come on, you Blades!

He obviously has no intention of being out-manoeuvred by a twelve-year-old and rises to his feet, having placed his hookah pipe safely underneath the goalpost.

Goo-on-den!
Goo-on-den!
Goo-on-den!

I take aim and shoot. I kick the ball as

hard as I can. Mohammed reaches forward and is just about to scoop the ball out of the air when, *crash!* Something falls out of the sky. Something large and bouncy. Mohammed is hit on the head by a bunch of over-ripened dates tumbling out of the goal post.

He isn't badly hurt but he stops and stands in a daze as the ball shoots past him, straight between the palm trees.

Y-e-e-e-e-ssss!

"Goal!!!" shout the Unitedites.

Two-one. Two-one. Two-one. Two-one.
United (Clap, clap, clap)
United (Clap, clap, clap)
United (Clap, clap, clap)

I can hardly believe it. I dash across the pitch, thumping the air with my fist, John Little style. The team crowd round:

Na na na na
He's a Blade and he's a Blade!

"Hoorah!" shout the supporters. "More! More!"

Take my hand
Take my whole life too.
Cos I can't help
falling in love with you.
United (Clap, clap, clap)

United (Clap, clap, clap)
United (Clap, clap, clap)

I get pats on the back from members of the team
and a big kiss on the cheek from Kelly.

> *You fill up my senses,*
> *like a gallon of Magnet,*
> *like a packet of Woodbines,*
> *like a good pinch of snuff.*
> *Like a night out in **Sheffield***
> *like a greasy chip butty,*
> *come, Sheffield United,*
> *come fill me again.*
> *La da da de ... ooo!*

Who would have thought that – only twelve years
old and playing as a keeper – I would already
have scored my first goal for Sheffield United?

Dear Rafiq,

Having a great time.
Played foottie on the beach + I
scored for United. The goats got
in the way but the camels made
very good goalposts.

It's dead hot. I've been swimming
underwater – though I didn't really
mean to – tell you when I get back.

Love,

George

CHAPTER
SEVENTEEN

On Day 3, I go with Grumps and Gramps on a trip to the local market.

Mohammed is waiting outside the hotel with a line of camels for us.

"Here we are!" says Grumps. "Personal taxi service. How about that then, eh?"

My camel kneels on the dusty ground so I can climb on to its back. I have to swing my leg across its hump, then sit on the stripy blanket and hold tight. The camel clambers to its feet, swaying and lurching from side to side.

At first, I seem so high in the air, I feel scared I might fall off. I swallow hard. "Hello, there," I whisper to the camel and give it a little pat. I'm surprised to find that it feels warm and soft and hairy.

"It's a grand day," Grumps shouts to Otto and Lotto.

"Here we go!" shouts Gramps as Mohammed helps her on to her camel with her shopping bag. "Over the hump!"

We lumber along in single file down the sandy track towards the market. The local women we pass are covered from head to foot in long black robes with only their eyes peering out. On their heads are balanced baskets piled with potatoes, dates and bananas. Men ride donkeys with baskets of fruit hanging over the sides. More donkeys pull creaking carts crammed with chickens and vegetables.

We dismount in the market square, ablaze with the colours of fruit and unfamiliar vegetables. The side roads are jammed with donkeys, motor bikes, mopeds and carts. The stalls are piled high with oranges and bananas. The air is heavy with the scent of spices.

"Do you think we could get a pot of tea?" asks Grumps.

I spot an open-air café across the square. "Over there." I point.

We thread our way through the maze of colourful stalls, past doorways where Arabs sit at low tables, hammering patterns on brass plates. We pass stalls selling perfume in fancy bottles, strange musical instruments and marzipan dates.

"Well, I'm ready for a sit-down," says Gramps.

We walk inside the café, where groups of Arabs are seated on low stools smoking hubble-bubble pipes. Arabian music is crackling from an old transistor radio balanced on the branch of a palm tree. Gramps, I notice, is the only woman in the café, but she doesn't seem to mind. "Do you think we could have a pot of tea for three?" I ask the waiter.

While we're waiting, I take my Tunisian money out of my pocket. I'd like to buy some presents while we're here, and I've already seen some things I want. "Will you be all right here for ten minutes?" I ask Grumps and Grumps. "I just want to nip across the road."

"Fifteen dinars," says the stallholder as I hold up a glass perfume bottle, painted with pink and yellow flowers.

It would make a lovely present for my mum, but fifteen dinars is far too much. I find a smaller bottle.

"Thirteen dinars."

I shake my head.

"This real gold." The man points to the gold-painted stopper. "This bottle real antique. Hand-painted."

I replace the bottle and pick up a cigarette lighter made of brass with a pattern of snakes and leaves, just right for my dad.

"Twelve dinar."

I shake my head again. I look at a box of

marzipan dates. I could afford those maybe, but only just.

I'm about to turn away, when a small voice says shyly, "Sheffield United."

I look up. There's a young boy, grinning at me from behind the stall. "Sheffield United," he repeats, pointing at my shirt.

"That's right," I tell him. I'm amazed that anyone has heard of Sheffield United over here. "The Blades."

The little boy walks out from behind the stall. He reaches out his hand and points to the crest of crossed Blades at the top of my shirt. "Sheffield United," he says again.

I nod and smile. "Sheffield United."

He gives a little tug on my shirt. "Come," he says. "I show you."

I hesitate. I don't know whether this is what my dad would call *going off with strange men*. I ought really to let Grumps and Gramps know where I am.

"Come. I show you." He tugs me again.

The boy is much younger than me. It's a bit silly to think that he might do me any harm. I shrug my shoulders and follow him.

"Me," he points to himself. "Ali."

"Ali," I repeat. "Me." I point to myself. "George."

"Gorge."

"No. J-J-Jeorge."

"Jaws."

I nod and grin. I think Jaws'll have to do.

Ali leads me to a small shack behind the stalls across the road. The shack is made out of palm leaves plaited together. It's about the same size as one of the stockrooms we have at school.

"Come."

There is no door, just an opening in the wall. The room is dark because there are no windows, but Ali lights the stub of a candle. "Come."

In the flicker of the candlelight, I can just make out a tiny table with an enamel bowl containing a bar of soap and a razor. There is no other furniture. There are coloured blankets folded neatly on the floor. There are no beds. Sacks have been made into pillows. There is no fireplace, no bathroom, no sink. There's a curtain across part of the room. It's made from a stripy blanket and held up with nails.

"Come, Jaws."

Ali lifts up the blanket and beckons.

I stand and stare around me. I point at the empty walls. I speak slowly and carefully. "Is this … " I point to Ali, " … where you live?"

He nods. "Ali live here. Also," he points to the five blankets and the five pillows by the wall. He tells me five more names.

I think of our house at home. The empty swimming pool. The Jacuzzi. The dishwasher and the microwave. The conservatory. The long, winding drive...

"Come, Jaws." Ali draws back the curtain and holds up the candle flame. I can hardly believe my eyes. There on the wall, fastened with drawing pins, creased and battered, is a picture torn out of a magazine. A team picture of Sheffield United.

My face breaks into a grin. "Sheffield United," I laugh.

"Yes," says Ali, smiling. "Sheffield United."

He points at my T-shirt. "Sheffield United." Then he points back at the picture. "Sheffield United."

Both of us grin together.

I look around this tiny part of the shack. In the corner on the floor is a clean shirt, a pair of jeans and some socks. On the floor is a sack and a blanket. I stand and shake my head in amazement. This tiny section behind the curtain, this must be Ali's room, I tell myself. These are his clothes. This picture of United is the only other thing he owns.

Ali and I are strangers, but I'm aware that he's shown me something very special, very personal. The picture is his prize possession.

I think of my own room with my big comfy bed, my own bathroom, my desktop, my books...

I feel a kind of choking, a lump in my throat as I look round the tiny space. This is something I want to stay with me. I want the memory to stay fixed in my mind. But there is nothing else to see. Only the shadowy space with the sack, the blanket, the pillow...

... and the picture of Sheffield United.

Ali leads me back to the market stall. Before I turn to leave, he reaches out again and touches my shirt.

I smile and nod.

The stallholder beckons me across. He's collected together the painted perfume bottle that I chose, the cigarette lighter and the marzipan dates and he's wrapping them in newspaper. Of course, I can't afford to buy all three of them. I start to shake my head.

Ali grips the bottom of my shirt again and points to the parcel, nodding his head. He gabbles to the stallholder in Arabic. I don't understand what's happening now. I start to feel a bit worried. I think I ought to be getting back to Grumps and Gramps.

Ali tugs on my shirt again. "Jaws," he says to me. "Jaws."

I nod.

"Ali." He points towards himself.

I nod again.

He points to the parcel, lifting my arm to encourage me to take it. He tugs at my shirt again. And that's when the penny drops.

My heart sinks. I start to shake my head.

Ali nods. The stallholder nods, thrusting the parcel towards me. I understand now what he's after. He wants me to give him my shirt.

I look away, embarrassed. How can I explain? How can I make him understand that this was the last shirt in the shop? This shirt cost nearly all my savings and it's the best shirt I've owned in all my life. A special holiday souvenir.

The stallholder is still thrusting the parcel towards me. It occurs to me now that he might be Ali's father. Obviously, with these items, he's trying to buy the shirt for him.

I don't know what to say. I don't know how to explain. I should have brought Gran's Sheffield Wednesday shirt with me. I wouldn't have minded trading that.

I look down at Ali, his lips squeezed tightly together as he stares up at the shirt.

The man behind the stall holds my gaze with an eager smile on his face. He points at my shirt.

I shake my head again. I look back at Ali's pleading face. I think of his ragged picture of the team, the most important thing he owns and I suddenly realize just how much the shirt would mean to him. I can buy another shirt, another time. I can go back to the Blades Shop any time I like. All I need is the money.

For Ali, this might be his only chance – the chance of a lifetime – to own a Sheffield United shirt. When I've gone, it'll be too late.

I look back down at Ali's lips, squeezed together in a pleading smile. I shrug my shoulders.

Then I reach out my hand and accept the little parcel wrapped tightly in Arabic newsprint. Ali looks up at me. His face is breaking into a huge, enormous grin.

I smile back at him. I place the parcel on the side of the stall, then nod my head at Ali as I begin to take off my shirt.

"Well, I'm not so sure about it being real gold," says Kelly, as she examines the stopper on the perfume bottle, "but the flowers are very nice."

"The perfume's lovely," says her mum, dabbing a tiny spot on her wrist and sniffing it. "It doesn't matter whether it's gold or not."

"That's what I thought."

> *Oh-oh-oh-oh the hokey cokey!*
> *Oh-oh-oh-oh the hokey cokey!*
> *Oh-oh-oh-oh the hokey cokey!*
> *Knees bend, arms stretch –*
> *Ya! Ya! Ya!!*

The tables and chairs have been pushed aside to make room for the circle of people, hopping across the sand:

> *You put your left leg in,*
> *Your left leg out.*
> *In. Out. In. Out.*
> *Shake it all about.*

Grumps raises her skirt above her knees, shaking her leg, can-can style. Cheers and wolf-whistles echo round the beach:

> *You do the hokey cokey*
> *and you turn around.*
> *That's what it's all about.*

It's now getting dark and turning cooler, but the bonfire is still burning and the hokey cokey keeps everyone warm.

> *Oh-oh-oh-oh the hokey cokey!*
> *Oh-oh-oh-oh the hokey cokey!*
> *Oh-oh-oh-oh the hokey cokey!*
> *Knees bend, arms stretch –*
> *Ya! Ya! Ya!!*

Jumping in and out causes a few collisions. This could be related to the fact the crate of beer that Otto bought now contains no more than empty bottles. Gramps and Lotto both look decidedly wobbly, but manage to stagger through the last few lines:

> *You put your whole self in*
> *Your whole self out.*
> *In. Out. In. Out.*
> *Shake it all about...*

"Oh dear! Oh dear!" says Grumps, mopping his forehead with his hankie. But he still staggers forward, walking-stick in hand:

> *You do the hokey cokey*
> *and you turn around.*
> *That's what it's all about.*

"Well, they're really enjoying themselves," says Kelly's mum.

I suddenly realize that Grumps and Gramps have transformed over the last two days. Instead of two very frail, elderly people who hardly know what day it is, they're now the life and soul of the party.

> *Oh-oh-oh-oh the hokey cokey!*
> *Oh-oh-oh-oh the hokey cokey!*
> *Oh-oh-oh-oh the hokey cokey!*
> *Knees bend, arms stretch –*
> *Ya! Ya! Ya!!*

"Old people just take longer to adjust," Kelly's mum explains, "especially when they're in a strange environment."

"They'll probably be just as bad again when they get home," Kelly giggles. "They'll go round to their next-door neighbours and ask them who they are. When they meet their daughter, they'll say, 'Well, it's a grand day. We've been for a ride on a camel, you know. Have we met you before at all?'"

"Shhhh!"

"We'll do the Conga next!" shouts Grumps, as he collapses into a chair. "Round all the chalets and the swimming pool."

Everyone groans. "We've no breath left."

"Hey," Gramps warns him, "remember, you've to be up early in the morning. You're goin' fishing with Assid."

"Anyway, it's a good job you came with them," says Kelly's mum.

"Well, I haven't done very much." I try not to laugh at Kelly, who's still impersonating Grumps, waving an imaginary walking-stick.

"Well, you've been here, giving them support. Everybody needs someone to hang on to."

"They'd still be riding round in circles in that pedalo if you weren't here," says Kelly. "'Ee, by gum, we're in a piccolo. Grab that there fish, Gramps. Grab that there sun 'at. 'Ee, it's a grand day, tha knows.'"

"Sshhh!"

Assid collects up the glasses. "Remember," he shouts to Grumps, "we go out in boat tomorrow. We catch big fish."

"That's right," says Grumps. "Trip round the bay, eh?"

"You'd better get to bed soon," says Gramps, "or you'll never get up in time."

As he passes our table Assid asks us, "You want coffee also, Jelly and Jaws?"

"*Kelly and George!*" we yell after him.

135

"And yes, please."

"I once went away on my own," says Kelly.

"Where did you go?"

"It was a sort of field course," Kelly explains, finishing her Coke. "Organized by the church – the youth club. It was a week of … like canoeing and rock climbing, that sort of thing. Mum thought it would be good for me."

"You weren't very keen though, were you?" her mum laughs.

"Well, it was with girls I didn't know all that well. I didn't fancy sharing a dormitory with them – not for a whole week."

"Did you enjoy it, though?"

"I had a fantastic time. It was exhausting – I've never felt as tired in my life. I ached in places I never knew I'd got. But I learned to steer a canoe, I went down potholes, climbed big rocks, abseiled over cliffs… The most amazing thing was, like, other people relying on me. I remember one day, I was holding this rope and another girl was on the other end and I just thought, *If I were to let go now*… I had somebody else's life right there in my hands. Somebody depending on me totally."

"It sounds great."

"Three cups of coffee." Assid places the tray down on our table, complete with sugar, cream and chocolate biscuits.

"How long you stay in Djerba?" he asks us.

136

"Eleven more days," Kelly tells him.

"That a long time."

"No." We shake our heads. "Not long enough."

"You no want go home?"

"No. We don't want to go home at all. We just want to stay here. Stay here for ever and ever."

— End of the Second Half —

INJURY
TIME

CHAPTER EIGHTEEN

But, of course, we cannot stay in Djerba for ever and the days pass very quickly.

Gayle, our travel rep, sits around with her feet up most of the two weeks because Grumps and Gramps organize so much entertainment down at The Happy Camel.

We don't book a trip to the oasis, but Mohammed arrives with his camels to take us to the carpet factory and to watch all the fishing boats arrive in the harbour. We don't bother with a Bedouin tent in the desert, but we do have picnics on the beach, a fancy dress party and an international 5-a-side World Cup.

"Will you fasten all seat belts, please, ready for take-off."

And now here we are, sitting on the plane ready to fly to Manchester. Time for the

stagecoach to change back into a pumpkin;
time for the team of white horses to change
back into mice.

"Please ensure that all seats are in the
upright position."

"Are you scared?" Kelly asks as we begin to
coast along the runway.

I turn away and stare out of the window as
the runway lights flick past.

"We hope you've enjoyed your holiday.
Captain Blake and his crew wish you all a
pleasant flight."

Kelly might have noticed that my lip is trem-
bling, but it isn't because I'm frightened.

"You may be interested to know that the
weather in Manchester is two degrees above
zero. It's been cloudy with outbreaks of rain
and snow on high ground..."

"Hey! Tell the pilot to turn the plane
round," shouts Grumps. "We're going back
for another week."

"Another fortnight," Gramps corrects him.

"Don't you want to go home?" Kelly asks.

I shake my head.

"You'll be glad to see your mum and dad
again, won't you? And everybody at school?"

I shrug my shoulders.

There will be some good things about it. I'll
be pleased to see Rafiq again and I'll enjoy
telling people all about the holiday.

"We'll be passing over the Mediterranean,

then coasting over the South of France…"

But as we accelerate down the runway, the wheels leave the ground, and the plane starts tipping skywards, something inside me starts to sink.

When I get home tomorrow morning, I'll wander round the house, checking all the familiar things: the cracked swimming pool and the dry Jacuzzi; the empty shell of a Mercedes Benz; the empty games room where the snooker table and the table tennis used to be…

"Did I tell you about when I came back from that field course?" Kelly asks.

"No. You told me about going on it."

"Well, I had a fantastic time. But then, when I came back home, I felt really strange. I felt as though I'd changed so much. You see, the course only lasted one week, but when I came home I felt about five years older. I'd learned so much. I expected everyone to treat me differently, but of course nobody did. It was just as though I'd grown up but everything else had stood still."

I gaze out of the window as the lights on the ground sink further and further below us.

"Hey, I think I can just spot The Happy Camel," shouts Gramps.

"Can you see Sid?" asks Grumps. "Is he waving us off?"

Of course, what Kelly says applies to me as well. When I get home, Mum and Dad will have already started sending back the things they bought with the holiday money. Much worse will be listening to my panic-stricken father, desperately trying to make up excuses over the phone when he can't keep up the payments. The house will slowly empty of all the nice things we bought and, without them, my mum and dad will get more and more anxious, more and more miserable, more and more cross.

And I'll think about Ali living in his shack, with his blanket and sack. And I will feel older and wiser because I've been somewhere, seen something that they don't even know about. And no matter how hard I try to explain, I know they won't understand.

"We've given Assid our address, you know," says Gramps. "We've invited him over next Christmas."

"And we're off to Germany in the summer. We're having two weeks with Otto and Lotto."

I haven't exactly held someone's life in my hands, the way Kelly did. But this week I've felt important. And when I get home I'll just be a twelve-year-old boy again that no one ever listens to. I'll feel empty inside. Like one of the empty storage units in my bedroom or the empty space where my TV and computer used to be. I'll feel just like a hollow container with the important things inside me wrenched away.

* * *

I fall asleep in Cherry's car. I wake up briefly to say goodbye to Grumps and Gramps but then I close my eyes again.

I don't want to talk. I don't want to look outside at the cold, drizzly rain. I don't want to see the covering of snow on top of the Pennine hills. I doze until we reach the end of our road, and then, as I open my eyes and see our house approaching, I realize with amazement that everything has changed.

First of all, there's a FOR SALE sign planted in the garden. Secondly, there's a light shining in our Victorian standard lamp. The wrought iron gates have been painted and, when we reach the house, the up-and-over garage doors are open. There's no sign of the Mercedes, but there are tea chests on the garage floor.

"It looks as if we're moving house," I murmur, rubbing my eyes.

Although it's still early in the morning, there are sounds of hoovering and hammering. When Mum appears, she's wearing a pair of denim dungarees and a headscarf. Dad is wearing paint-splashed jeans and an oily sweatshirt. "Can we offer you some coffee?" he asks Cherry.

"No, thanks. I've got to get back and see to Grumps and Gramps." She hesitates. "They've had a wonderful time. They say your George was an absolute godsend." She beams down at me. "I just want to thank you for allowing him to go."

"Well, I've enjoyed it," I tell her. "I had a lovely time."

"Well, you'd better come in and tell us all about it," says Mum.

So many things have happened in the last two weeks, there's so much I want to tell them that the words get stuck inside my throat.

"Listen," says Dad, "before you start. There's a few things we ought to tell you." He pours us both a mug of filtered coffee. I'm surprised, of course, that the coffee machine hasn't been returned by now. We must have had it at least three weeks.

"There's been some changes while you've been away." He glances outside towards Grandma, wearing a pair of Mum's leggings, fur boots, an old jumper and a Balaclava hat. She has a bucket and trowel and appears to be cementing the cracks in the swimming pool.

"We've been very concerned about Grandma," Mum explains. "People her age sometimes start to lose their brain a bit. They call it getting senile."

I don't say anything.

"We've come to the conclusion that Grandma isn't really capable of coping now that Grandad's gone."

I pour some cream into my coffee. "It could be the strange environment," I explain.

"People take longer to adjust to new places when they're older."

Dad nods, but looks puzzled at my new wisdom. "Anyway," he says, "we decided that we ought to let Gran stay with us. It wasn't an easy decision because, well … she can be a bit annoying sometimes."

At this moment, Gran peeps her head round the door of the conservatory. She grins inanely and waves her trowel in the air. "You *can* go to the ball," she tells me.

"We thought the best thing," Mum explains as Gran floats across the patio, waving her cement-encrusted wand, "would be to sell this house and buy somewhere smaller. Somewhere with a granny flat. That's like separate accommodation but built into the same house."

I have been suggesting for the last eighteen months that if we moved into a smaller, cheaper house all our financial problems would be solved. Now Mum and Dad are talking as if it was their idea.

"Your gran's very keen," says Dad. "In fact, she's offered to help out financially. That means we can afford to move into a new place without having to wait for someone else to buy this one."

"Anyway," Mum explains, "we found an ideal place right away. The first place we looked at. I'm sure you'll like it, George."

"It's a lot smaller than we're used to, of course," says Dad. "It hasn't got a swimming pool but," he glances at me with a little twinkle in his eye, "it is within walking distance of your favourite football club…"

EXTRA
TIME

CHAPTER NINETEEN

The world is striped in red and white as we head towards Bramall Lane. Red and white striped shirts, red and white striped bowler hats, red and white scarves and red and white painted faces.

We'll follow United
over land and sea,
We will follow United
on to victory.
United!
United!
United!

The crowd thickens along London Road. The cars become blocked on Woodhead Road. Fans queue at John Sanella's ice-cream van and the hot dog van. There's another queue for badges and souvenirs. Another queue for programmes. But the biggest queue of all is the queue to get into the ground.

Blades men, super Blades men,
We are Blades men, from the Lane...

Rafiq and I clutch our red and white balloons and our tickets for the Kop. We make our way along Shoreham Street, through the turnstile and up the steps, where already there's a thunderous chanting:

And it's Sheffield United,
Sheffield United F.C.
are by far the greatest team
the world has ever seen.

My nostrils quiver with the aroma of hot meat pies. I can afford one now – now that Gran buys me tickets for the match and I'm getting pocket money again. Because now we've moved into our smaller house, now Dad's sold the empty Mercedes and bought a bike, we can afford nice food, hot water, central heating and lots of treats. I cradle my pie, piping hot in its silver tray, as we scour the tiers of seats to find our places.

United!
United!
United!

We sit high up behind the goal, gazing at the red and white sea below us. At the swelling red and white waves along the South Stand and the John Street Stand. Then, across the pitch, at the distant tiers of Everton Blues.

I bite into my pie as today's team flashes on to the electronic scoreboard:

1. Callum Welly
11. Alan Ward

The crust is crisp and tasty, warm and soggy in the centre and dripping with gravy:

33. Roger Nelson
22. Sandy Cott
12. John Little

And then the great Blades flag appears, billowing like a huge marquee, covering the crowd. Our hands reach out, drawing the sail above our heads and all the world is red, like a huge crimson cave. A scarlet universe as two thousand United fans are stacked inside one stripe. Then the sky lifts and the world is light again, white as a snowstorm. Then red again. Then daylight. I look down towards the pitch, where Everton are already kicking the ball and then – a massive cheer. We rise to our feet as one body.

"Ra-a-a-a...!"

First the mascots carrying the ball and then the team. Ryan Bayle, Wayne Dytehouse.

Rafiq and I both have our hands clasped around the same tangle of string. We let go together as a thousand red and white balloons soar with one motion like a flock of birds suddenly disturbed. We gaze at our small cluster of balloons, floating upwards, until they're absorbed inside the cloud of red and white.

"Come on, you Reds!"

Players run around the pitch, leaping on to bouncing bundles of balloons. Pop. Pop. Pop. Pop.

Come on, you Reds!

Pop. Pop. Pop.

You fill up my senses
like a gallon of Magnet,
like a packet of Woodbines,
like a good pinch of snuff.

Pop. Pop. Pop.

Like a night out in Sheffield
like a greasy chip butty.

Pop. Pop. Pop.

Come Sheffield United,
come fill me again.
La da da de...ooo!

Pop. Pop. Pop.
Time to take our seats.
Some people think football fans are

hooligans. They think we come here to cause trouble and get into fights. They think we're the stupid kids who are no good at school, who can hardly read or write. They think we spend the rest of our week walking round the streets, beating up old ladies. Some people think being a football supporter is a complete waste of time.

> *Oh, we ain't got a barrel of – money.*
> *We ain't got Woodward or – Currie.*
> *But we're rolling along*
> *Singing our song,*
> *United.*

I often think of what Kelly's mum said about everybody needing someone to hang on to. Needing somebody there to support them. Sheffield United have some of the best supporters in the country. The Blades know we'll always be there, backing them, whether they win or lose, whether they go up or down.

Suddenly, we rise to our feet because there's a corner and this could be our first chance for a goal. Standing, with our fists thrust into the air we chant:

> *Goo-on-den!*
> *Goo-on-den!*
> *Goo-on-den!*
> *Bip bip bibibip bibibibibibeep...*

And Ryan Bayle's header goes straight through to Sandy Cott, who shoots towards the net and ... *Ye-e-e-e-e-ss!!*

The electronic scoreboard flashes:

GOAL!
GOAL!
GOAL!

as its digital football explodes into an imaginary net. And it shows the new score:

Sheffield United.....1
Everton..............0

Rafiq and I throw our arms around each other. We dance up and down. We thrust our fists into the air.

Davy Bassett's red and white army,
Davy Bassett's red and white army.
Bip bip bibibip bibibibibibeep.

For the first time since the game started, there's an inert silence from the Blues at the Everton end of the ground. But we are jumping and dancing and applauding until the ball is returned to the centre. Then it's everyone back to their seats.

Of course, today it doesn't particularly matter whether we win or lose. The relegation battle has all been sorted out and there are no more cup matches left. We just want to win because that's what football's all about.

And it's Sheffield United,
Sheffield United F.C.
are by far the greatest team
the world has ever seen...

I remember the day my dad said to me, *You wouldn't want to support a team, would you, that had been relegated to the first or the second division?*

I thought a lot about that. It was after I'd suggested that we move into a smaller house. *You see, George,* I remember Dad saying, *we're used to the premier division.*

I thought about it a lot because it shows the difference between my dad and me.

You see, the way I look at it, when you support somebody, you support them through thick and thin, good or bad. There are some fans who support United only when they're doing well. There are some who only turn out when the weather's good; there are others who only come to a match when it's not being shown on TV.

The only thing that's prevented me from getting to a match is not having any money. But, even then, I still supported the team. I still cared about them. I still stuck up for them if anybody slagged them off.

United!
United!
United!

157

The same with our family. I still stuck up for them when we didn't have any money. I didn't moan when my father hadn't got a job. I tried not to complain when we were poor – even when I was hungry.

Na, na, na, na,
He's a Blade an' he's a Blade.

We rise to our feet again as John Little takes possession and takes on the Everton defence. He makes a long, sweeping pass to Wayne Dytehouse, who's lost his marker on the edge of the penalty area. Wayne makes an emphatic shot towards the goal and … *Ye-e-e-e-e-ss!!*

GOAL!
GOAL!
GOAL!
Bip bip bibibip bibibibibibeep…
Two-nil
two-nil
two-nil
two-nil…

We sing together because, as I was saying, I support United through thick and thin, I support them if they win or lose. I support them if they stay up or go down.

Take my hand
Take my whole life too
'cos I can't help
falling in love with you…

That's what loyalty's all about. Someone's hand there, reaching out, someone to support you, someone you can hang on to.

That's what it means to be a loyal fan. And that's what it means to be a true supporter of United.

The best team in the world.